THE CASE OF THE KILLER DIVORCE

DIVORCE

JAMIE QUINN COZY MYSTERIES BOOK 2

BARBARA VENKATARAMAN

ACKNOWLEDGMENTS

For all of their support, advice and enthusiasm, I want to thank all of my "reader girls:" Janet, Jaya, Jodi, Joette, Leslie, Linda, Myra and Nanette.

CHAPTER 1

"WITH ALL DUE RESPECT, YOUR HONOR--" I INTERRUPTED, desperate to keep my client out of jail. I knew better than to argue with a judge, but still, I had to try.

"Counselor," Judge Marcus said, clearly annoyed. "We all know what 'with all due respect' means--it means you think I'm dead wrong. I've made my ruling Miss Quinn, *this hearing is over.*"

With that, the judge stood up and exited the courtroom, black robe flapping in his wake. He'd made it clear that I was done talking--at least to him.

God, I hate being a lawyer, I thought, not for the first time. My client, Becca Solomon, was seated next to me looking worried and confused. She had no clue what just happened, but she knew it was bad.

I turned my chair so I could face her. "I'm sorry, Becca, the judge denied our motion. *That means you have to let Joe take the kids on Friday.* If you refuse, the judge will hold you in contempt and you could wind up in jail. He's not happy with you--and he likes me even less."

My client covered her face with her hands and began to cry, shoulders shaking, head down, trying to shut out a world that, in her mind, refused to protect her children. I pulled a tissue from my purse and offered it to her. Divorce lawyers always have tissues handy--it's a tool of the trade you don't learn about in law school. You also don't learn how gut-wrenching it is to practice family law.

After taking a deep breath, Becca regained control. She looked around to make sure Joe and his lawyer had left. Since her arrival at the courthouse, her appearance had changed drastically, going from a well-put-together grad student to a wild-eyed, disheveled fugitive ready to bolt.

I'd seen that haunted look before. My name is Jamie Quinn and after ten years of practicing law, I've seen it all. You wouldn't think a sleepy town like Hollywood, Florida would have much drama, but it does. The judge who swore me in had warned me, saying, 'You'll never believe what goes on between four walls,' and he was right; it's unbelievable. Take my client, Carol (*please take her; you'd make me so happy*). She and her husband are well-off, successful in their respective careers, and dress like they're posing for a fashion magazine, yet they have screaming matches in front of their kids and pour pitchers of Kool-Aid on each other. Then there was the vengeful couple--I forget their names--who took turns living in the marital home, escalating the damage to the house each time they switched, just to piss each other off. It started when the husband removed all the light bulbs and fixtures, and ended when the wife took out all the sinks and toilets. I figured they'd wind up killing each other, like Kathleen Turner and Michael Douglas in 'The War of the Roses', but I was wrong. They remarried.

I turned my attention back to Becca Solomon, who was having a meltdown. I remember the first time she walked into my office. I thought she looked like a model: Scandinavian blonde with wide blue eyes and a sprinkling of freckles on her nose that made her look younger than twenty-five. She was educated and poised and made a convincing witness. At least that's what I thought. Apparently, Judge Marcus didn't agree.

Becca's story was hardly unusual--she'd met a new guy and wanted out of her marriage. Her mistake was assuming it would be easy. Getting a divorce isn't like changing banks or firing your pool boy, it's a whole lot messier, especially when you have kids. And while new love is wonderful and romantic, it's not real life. Eventually, someone has to pay the bills, get up with the baby, and take out the trash. I don't mean a person should never start over, I'm just saying 'new' doesn't always mean 'improved.' Everyone you meet has emotional baggage--even me. Honestly, if I had any more baggage, I could start my own airline.

But, back to Becca, all she wanted was a divorce and primary custody of her two young daughters, and, of course, child support. Also, alimony and attorney's fees and half the marital assets. And one last thing--she wanted to continue living in her palatial home with her children, plus bring in her boyfriend, Charlie Santoro. If only her husband, Joe, weren't causing so much trouble. I know that makes her sound selfish and awful, but, to be fair, Florida is a no-fault state which means, if you want a divorce, you get it, and things like infidelity don't matter at all. The courts treat marriage more like a financial partnership. Wasting assets is always considered relevant, but your emotional state, not so much.

To say that Joe was angry is like saying Hurricane Katrina was just a little bad weather. And it didn't help that Becca's new love, Charlie, used to be Joe's friend. They say that criminal lawyers see bad people on their best behavior and divorce lawyers see good people at their worst, and it's true. Joe seemed like a decent enough guy, but he spent a lot of time trying to punish Becca. His favorite threat was that he'd take the kids away from her.

Becca had finally calmed down when the judge's bailiff, Harold, started pointing at his watch.

"Hate to kick you out, Jamie, but we have another hearing coming in."

"I've been kicked out of better places than this," I joked as I packed up my briefcase.

Harold laughed at that and even Becca smiled a little. We stood up and turned to leave right when Joe sauntered back into the room, looking smug."

"You'd better get used to this, Becca," he said, a sneer distorting his boyish face. "Because when the judge finds out about you, he's going to give me custody."

Becca stared him down, cold as ice. "If you try to take my kids away, I swear to God, Joe, I will kill you."

CHAPTER 2

"Do I need to call security?" the bailiff asked, wagging his finger at Becca and Joe. Harold had to be at least seventy-five years old, but he was a retired cop and he wasn't putting up with any nonsense from these two. He had a court-room to run.

I hissed at Becca not to get into it with Joe, then took her by the arm and pulled her towards the door. Divorce work can be so unpleasant. I often wonder why I went to law school just to end up as a glorified babysitter. I actually took a break from lawyering about two years ago when my mom died of cancer. I was such a wreck that even after six months of doing nothing, I still couldn't pull myself together. It took my autistic cousin, Adam, being accused of murder to snap me out of it. Not only did I finally leave my house, but I also left my comfort zone, which was kind of terrifying. Exhilarating, but terrifying. To tell you the truth, I couldn't wait to do it again.

As I nudged Becca towards the central elevators in the middle of the courthouse, I was aware of what an odd pair we made, her with her Nordic beauty, at least 5'9" before she put on her heels, and me, 5'2" if I stood up straight, olive skin of unknown heritage, and dark curly hair that refused to cooperate. In the elevator, I counseled Becca that she shouldn't let Joe get to her; that he was trying to make her angry and that she was giving him what he wanted.

"But, Jamie," she said, her eyes brimming with tears, "We're talking about my girls! If I don't protect them, who will?"

"I understand that you're worried, but it's all going to be fine. The girls are entitled to have their dad in their lives. If he steps out of line, the judge will come down hard on him. Are you keeping a log of everything that happens, like I told you to?"

She nodded mutely. The elevator had reached the lobby and people were trying to push their way in before we could get out. Nice!

I patted Becca on the arm, reassuringly. "I have to stop at the Clerk's office now, okay? We'll talk soon. Can you find your way back to your car?"

Becca nodded again. Her pale face looked otherworldly under the fluorescent lights. As she walked away, oblivious to the buzzing crowd around her, I suddenly had a bad feeling about her, but I shrugged it off.

Stop it, Jamie! Next thing you know, you'll be buying Tarot cards and a Ouija board...

I trudged back up to the Clerk's office to argue about some lost paperwork.

CHAPTER 3

It felt strange to be back in my office after taking so much time off. When I was on hiatus, I was never sure what day it was, but it didn't matter anyway since I had nowhere to be. The truth is I hardly left my house--the house my mom passed on to me--unless I had to, but now it felt good to have a reason to get up every morning and people who needed me--although I missed having a wide open calendar. There was so much possibility in those white spaces. Not that I ever took advantage of it.

Don't get me wrong, I was pretty stressed when I was dealing with my mom's death, but it was a different kind of stress. Back then, I was completely self-absorbed in my grief; now, I was stressed because everyone wanted a piece of me. Speaking of stress, allow me to introduce you to Lisa. She's the receptionist for our shared office space and a new addition, hired while I was away. She's also a hot mess. Lisa's very sweet, but not the brightest bulb in the chandelier. That doesn't bother me as much as her tendency to cry the minute anything goes wrong. She also cries if she thinks something *might* go wrong. And sometimes she cries when she talks to her fiancé on the phone. I only have so much patience, which I need to reserve for my clients. There isn't enough to cover Lisa, too.

You'd think my contact with her would be limited, since all she does for me is take phone messages and hand me my mail-- she doesn't even have to open it. Somehow though, I am still subjected to her tears at least once a day. Before you conclude that the poor girl must be depressed, I'll tell you that I've considered that, but she doesn't *act* depressed; she seems fine. I was baffled by Lisa until I read an article about adults who continue using childhood defense mechanisms to deal with their problems. Ah, that explains it! Now, if I could only find an article on how to make her stop crying.

I was back at my desk after my tough morning with Becca. I hated losing in court, every lawyer does, but I take it to heart. You could say I obsess about it, which doesn't help my chronic insomnia one bit. I suppose I need *something* to think about when I'm up at three in the morning, but those sure aren't billable hours.

There was a knock at my office door followed by a giggle.

"Come in."

"There's someone here to see you, Jamie."

Lisa looked happier than I'd ever seen her, eyes bright, a blush highlighting her round cheeks. Even her hair looked perkier. She glanced over her shoulder and giggled again.

"He said his name is *Marmaduke!*"

"That's right, Sugar, Marmaduke Broussard, the Third, at your service." Duke flashed a smile at Lisa, then walked right in and sat down.

"Jamie, why didn't you tell me you had such a hot receptionist? I would've been here sooner," Duke said.

Lisa was overcome by a fit of giggles and blushes.

I laughed. "No hitting on the staff, Duke. Besides, Lisa's taken, she's about to get married."

"Excellent!" Duke said. "But if you change your mind, Darlin', you let me know." He winked at her salaciously.

I waved her away and Lisa reluctantly closed the door.

"I'm amazed that you don't get beat up by jealous boyfriends on a daily basis," I said, grinning at my former client, now friend. I'd rescued Duke from his angry ex-wife and he'd helped me big-time when my cousin Adam was in trouble.

"As long as I can run faster than them, I'll be alright," he joked.

Duke had a way with the ladies, which is how he'd been married three times. He looked pretty good for a guy who spent all his spare time drinking at a bar called 'The Big Easy.' Picture a pirate-type, around thirty-five, shoulder length brown hair, perfect teeth, and laughing green eyes. He always wore a shark-tooth necklace and his favorite alligator boots. You've probably seen him. As a private investigator, he gets around.

I pushed aside the stack of files on my desk so we could see each other. Also, with the files out of sight, I didn't have to feel guilty about the work I wasn't doing.

"Do you have any news for me, Duke? Or did you just come by to flirt with our receptionist?" I teased.

"Ouch, Jamie! You know I come here to see you. Actually, I was hoping you'd buy me lunch, I'm starving."

"Sure, I'd love to get out of here. You like Thai? There's a new place a few blocks away." I grabbed my purse.

Sounds great," he said, pushing his chair back to stand up. "And while we're there, I can tell you about my brilliant detective work."

"Don't tell me you know where my father is!" I couldn't keep the excitement out of my voice.

"Buy me lunch and you'll find out."

CHAPTER 4

"Why are you so mean?"

We were driving to *Try My Thai* in my Mini Cooper and Duke wouldn't answer a single one of my questions.

"Why are you so impatient?" he countered. "We'll be there in about ten seconds. Man, I hope they have 'Jumping Shrimp' and then I hope those suckers jump right into my mouth! I see you laughing over there, you think I'm funny."

"As long as you amuse yourself, that's all that matters," I said, parking the car. "Let's go, Mr. Hilarious."

The food came out soon after we ordered and we dug right in. "Start talking, Duke," I said. "Or *you're* buying *me* lunch."

Duke inhaled deeply. "This stuff smells as great as it tastes, and it's damn spicy too! Good choice." He gave me a wicked smile in between scarfing down his food.

I could see he was planning to drag this out.

"Did you notice the décor?" I asked. "How all the pictures on the wall are made from silk ties--isn't that fun?"

"Sure is. You going to eat that spring roll?"

I shook my head and handed it to him. "Which tie is your favorite, Duke?"

He looked around, "I don't know, maybe that orange one, it looks like a bad acid trip," he said, laughing. "Why are you askin'?"

"Because that's the tie I'm going to strangle you with if you don't tell me something soon."

Duke started laughing so hard, I thought he was going to choke on his food. "You should see your face, Jamie, no...wait, here we go..."

Before I knew what he was doing, Duke had taken my picture with his phone. He showed it to me and I started laughing, too. He fiddled with the phone for a minute, and then he said, "There--now every time you call me, that picture's going to pop up. I can't wait!"

I wiped my eyes; laughing and spicy foods always get to me. "Listen buddy, if you start choking again, I'm not saving you."

"Then you'll never know what I was going to tell you."

"True enough," I said, calmly finishing off my Vegetable Panang.

"Okay," he said, "That was fun, but I'm done torturing you. First off, I have to say, you didn't give me much to go on. I mean, you said your Dad's name was Bill Frank, and that's not even his real name."

"What??"

"Hang on, Jamie, I'm gettin' there. I started with the easy stuff. He's not registered to vote in any state, he's got no driver's license in Florida, and there's no marriage license either-- since your parents weren't married."

"So, what did you do next?" I was hanging on Duke's every word, and he knew it.

"I remembered you said your mom met him at a political protest in Miami, and that they were both arrested. It took me a long time to figure it out, but I finally matched an arrest record. Your dad's real name is *Guillermo Franco* and he's not even an American citizen, he's Cuban"

"Wow, Duke! You're amazing! Where is he now? What's he doing? Where's he been all this time? Oh my God, I don't even know where to start..." I was crying again, this time for real.

Duke was shaking his head warily, flustered by my tears. "I'm sorry, Darlin', I don't know any of that yet. I'm still working on it. But I do have something to show you." He reached into his pocket, pulled out a piece of paper and handed it to me.

As I unfolded it, I realized what it was. A man with wavy black hair and olive skin was posing for the camera. I had a weird sensation, like I was looking into my own eyes. I finally had a picture of my father.

CHAPTER 5

IT WAS SURREAL TO BE HOLDING A PHOTO OF MY FATHER after I'd spent so many years imagining him. This is going to sound dumb but, when I was little, I used to look for him everywhere--in crowds, on TV, in school. He might've been anyone, and it was up to me to find him. It was a game I used to play: if I recognized him, then he would stay. Of course, I never did find him, and it made me feel incomplete somehow, unfinished, like a jigsaw puzzle with missing pieces. Nobody could understand how I felt, not even my friends whose parents were divorced because they at least had two parents. Now the game was over and it turned out my father was the same person he'd always been, an ordinary guy who didn't want to be my dad. I mean, why hadn't he made an effort to find *me* in the last thirty-three years? It's not like I was hiding, I'd been living in Hollywood since the day I was born.

"Aren't you going to say something?" Duke asked. "I can't believe what I'm seeing--Jamie the lawyer's at a loss for words!"

I couldn't help it; I burst into tears and escaped to the bathroom, leaving Duke at the table with his mouth hanging open.

As I stood over the sink crying my eyes out, part of me was still rational enough to wonder what I'd hoped to accomplish by looking for my dad. I'd pretended it was simply a mystery to solve, a way to satisfy my lifelong curiosity, but that wasn't true. I'd been searching because I needed to know who I was and where I came from. The problem was with that little girl. She was still playing the game, still trying to find her dad, even if he broke her heart in the end.

"You okay in there?" Duke was standing outside the bathroom door. Poor guy, he'd done so much for me and I'd totally freaked out on him.

"Sorry if I upset you," he went on. "You know, being half-Cuban's not so bad--I think Cuban girls are hot!"

That made me laugh. Leave it to Duke to get it all wrong. He only knew one way of looking at things, that was for sure. I washed my face and blew my nose before opening the door.

"I forgot to tell you that spicy food makes me cry," I said, trying to keep a straight face.

"Well, that seems like a pretty important piece of information, Jamie. If that's how it's going to be, then, damn it, I'm picking the restaurant next time." Duke gave me a wink. Maybe he didn't have it wrong after all.

It had been a very eventful day--and it was only half over. I paid the bill and we headed back to my office.

CHAPTER 6

I SPENT THE AFTERNOON AT MY DESK RETURNING CALLS and drafting pleadings, but my mind was elsewhere, preoccupied with the riddle of my father. Duke offered to keep digging around, but I asked him to hold off for a while. After my embarrassing meltdown at lunch, maybe I wasn't ready to hear it. Or maybe the best thing to do was to plow through and resolve this nagging problem for good. I couldn't think straight anymore. I spent so much time giving advice to my clients and helping them make decisions that I was too burnt out to deal with my own stuff. What I needed was some perspective, some distance, and possibly some psychoanalysis, but, most of all, I needed a good laugh. What I needed was my friend, Grace. The best way to chat with Grace during the day was by text. She worked in Fort Lauderdale for a big securities firm that kept her busy, but she could usually answer a text.

Hola Amiga! Guess what I found out today? BTW, I just gave you a clue...

Hmmm...you like to eat at Chipotle? You're dying for a Frozen Margarita?

Not even close, Grace...

Give me another clue.

I'm thinking of taking salsa & merengue lessons because it's in my "blood."

You're auditioning for "Dancing with the Stars?" I got it-- you're a Cuban vampire!

You're half-right...

You're a vampire?? Wow, Jamie!!

This isn't 'Twilight', Grace. No, I found out my dad is Cuban.

You're kidding! A Cuban named Bill Frank?

A/K/A Guillermo Franco

Awesome! What else did you find out?

Nada. Not sure if I want to know more.

Don't be a chicken! Of course you do! Isn't there someone your mom was close to back then?

How do I know? I wasn't born yet. Lol

Think, James! Even I can think of someone...

I'm totally clueless.

What about her sister?? You know, your Aunt Peg?

Peg's never mentioned my father.

I bet you never asked.

Nope, never have.

Do it! Then we can go out for Cuban food and celebrate your heritage.

Alright, I guess...

Hasta la vista baby

Yeah yeah

It couldn't hurt to talk to Peg; I owed her a phone call anyway. After my mom died a year ago, we didn't see much of each other because we were both grieving in our own way. But when her son, Adam, was accused of murder, that brought us back together pretty quick. Now, I tried to have dinner with them at least once a month so we could catch up.

I decided to pack it up early and go home. It had been a tough day and I could feel a headache blooming behind my eyes. I popped two aspirin and speed-dialed my aunt on my cell. I could walk and talk without tripping most of the time. After we chatted about how Adam was doing at Broward College and how much Aunt Peg loved her new class of second-graders, she asked what was new with me. It made me catch my breath, how much she sounded like my mom. I was afraid I might start crying again, but I choked it down.

"Is everything okay?" she asked, concerned.

"I'm fine, no worries. Can I ask you something, Aunt Peg?"

"Of course, Jamie."

"Well, um, I was wondering...do you know anything about my father?"

There was a long moment of silence, so long that I thought we'd been disconnected.

"Yes," she finally answered, "And I have something for you that I've been holding for quite a while."

"Now I'm curious, what is it?"

"If you come over, I'll show you."

CHAPTER 7

I DON'T REMEMBER DRIVING TO MY AUNT'S HOUSE. FOR ALL I know, the car drove itself there. On the way, I kept wondering why I'd never asked Aunt Peg about my father, considering that she and my mother had been so close. My mom had always been protective of her younger sister, especially later, when Peg's divorce left her completely devastated and caring for an autistic son on her own. I'm sure Peg also helped my mom through some rough times, but I was too young to remember. I suppose when you know someone your whole life, it never occurs to you to ask them questions about their past. It would feel weird, like you were interviewing them for a magazine, or like you were just being nosy. Mostly, you assume you already know everything about them. But, as I'm learning, everyone has their secrets.

Aunt Peg greeted me at the door with a hug and invited me into her cozy living room where we sat down together on the overstuffed sofa.

"Jamie, I made a promise to your mom and I've kept it,

although it was difficult. She wanted you to know who your father is, but not until you were ready."

"That's ridiculous! So, you were never going to tell me anything unless I asked?"

She looked down at her hands folded in her lap and didn't say anything.

I jumped up and started pacing. "What am I, a child? I'm thirty-three years old, Aunt Peg! I think I can handle whatever it is. What's the story? Is he a drug dealer? A war criminal? I mean--what the hell?"

I sat down again. "I'm sorry, it's not your fault and I shouldn't take it out on you."

My aunt gave me a little smile. "It's alright, Jamie. I would've done the same--or worse. But I'm glad I can finally give you this. It's a letter from your mom."

I was not expecting that. It had been hard enough to listen to my mom's voice on my answering machine after she died; how could I possibly read a letter from her? I carefully unfolded the letter and made myself read slowly, fighting the urge to race through it and devour every word. Seeing her beautiful handwriting tore me up almost as much as her words did.

May 8, 2012

My dearest Jamie,

It feels so strange to be writing you a letter when you're right here, sleeping in the next room. I just realized that I've never written to you before and I'm sorry that this will be my first and last letter to you; it's like a sappy movie on the Lifetime channel.

We've always been able to talk to each other about anything, with one exception, and that's my fault. Jamie, I can't tell you how sorry I am that I never told you about your father. I still can't bring myself to do it in person--even now that time is running out. It's selfish of me, I know, but I never wanted to hurt you, and I still don't.

When you were little, you used to ask about your father constantly. It was painful for me to have to lie to you. Eventually, you stopped asking, and that caused me pain, too, but for a different reason. I always planned to talk to you about him, but it never seemed like the right time. I'm sure your mind is racing now, imagining all kinds of things, so let me put you at ease, your father is a good man and I regret every day that he can't be a part of your life.

His name is Guillermo Franco, but he used to go by Bill Frank. We met in 1978 at a political rally in Miami that my friend Carmen convinced me to go to. Carmen is Cuban and still had family over there. She was very passionate about their cause. Things were bad for Cubans, both at home and in the U.S., where they had fled to take refuge from Castro's regime. That was the year Cuban exiles In New York bombed the Cuban Mission to the United Nations. It was a tense time.
The minute I got to the rally, I wanted to leave. It was total chaos and it didn't help that I couldn't speak Spanish. When I lost Carmen in the crowd, I panicked. I was getting pushed and shoved from every direction until someone stepped in and started pushing people away from me. I turned around and found myself looking into the kindest eyes I'd ever seen. He was only twenty, like me, but he seemed so sure of himself. He told me to stay close, that he'd keep me safe, and I believed him. Bill was a stranger, but I trusted him immediately. Even when the police came and we were arrested, he was still looking out for me.

After we were released the next day, Bill and I started spending a lot of time together. Our relationship was all the more intense because of the political upheaval and Bill's involvement in the Cuban cause. We were together for a year and we were incredibly happy, but then, on June 11, 1979, everything fell apart. Several Cubans tried to force their way into the Venezuelan Embassy and the police opened fire. One person was wounded and the others were arrested, including Bill. They deported him and I never saw him again. A month later, I found out I was pregnant with you.

All these years, I kept hoping to hear from him, but I never did. I can only assume he's dead or in prison. So, you see, that's not a nice story to tell a little girl about her daddy. I couldn't even invent a happy ending, so I kept it to myself.

Bill was (is?) a wonderful person and you would've loved him, as he would've loved you. I know that you always wished you had a dad and I'm sorry I couldn't give you yours. I see a lot of him in you: his kindness, his sense of humor and his ability to relate to all kinds of people. And he liked to read science fiction, just like you do.

I hope you can forgive me, Jamie. I wish things could've been different, but that's how it goes. You are the most important person in my life and I'm so grateful to have you for a daughter. I think you already know that.

All my love,
Mom

CHAPTER 8

I READ THE LETTER TWICE, TRYING TO MAKE THE WORDS stick in my brain, but they kept breaking apart. I couldn't seem to wrap my head around the concepts. Things like *prison, dead, no happy ending*-- they couldn't be true, I didn't want them to be true. All my life, I'd been looking for a man who wasn't there, who didn't even know I existed.

"You look so pale, Jamie. Are you alright?" my aunt asked. "I know it's a lot to--"

"I'm sorry," I said, "I have to go."

She took my hand and squeezed it. "Why don't you stay for dinner? Adam will be home soon with the dogs. I know he'd love to see you."

I shook my head. "I can't, Aunt Peg. I need to be alone right now."

On the short drive to my house on Polk Street, I tried to clear my head and think about nothing. When that didn't work, I did the only meditation exercise I knew, focusing on my breathing while repeating, "I am breathing in, I am breathing out." Before I knew it, I was home. Being home usually makes me feel better, but when I opened the door, there he was, Mr. Paws. Along with inheriting my mom's house, I'd also inherited her cat, a cat that went out of his way to make me feel unwelcome. When I used to visit my mom, he would hiss at me and I'd hiss right back. My mom would just laugh and say, "Can't you two get along?"

Now that I was the person feeding him, he'd stopped hissing, but that didn't mean we liked each other. I'd changed his name to "Mr. Pain in the Ass," to match his personality, which didn't make him like me any less, but only because that wasn't possible.

After I fed the ungrateful creature, I tried to watch TV, but I couldn't focus. I wasn't hungry, so I decided to take a shower and go to bed. Not that I expected to sleep much (sleeping is not my forte), but I was bone-tired and needed a break from the real world.

If this were a movie of my life, the script would read 'cut to dream sequence' and then a bizarre scene would unfold...

I'm in a crowd looking for my father. I know he's there, but I can't find him. Everyone is taller than me and some people have animal faces, which scares me. They push and shove past me like I'm invisible. Someone is yelling, but I can't understand anything. I am starting to panic and then I see a woman who looks familiar. I try to get her attention and, suddenly, she's standing next to me. It's Becca Solomon, but she looks different. Her eyes are black, like fish eyes, and there's blood on her clothes. She says "I warned him, but he wouldn't listen" and then she's gone. The crowd thins out; a man is walking towards me. He doesn't look like my father, but somehow I know it's him. I feel like I can breathe again. He smiles at me and the crowd disappears

I wake up feeling rested and at peace. My left side feels warmer than my right, which seems odd until I realize that the cat has crawled into bed with me and is purring softly. I pet him and he nuzzles my hand. My life just gets stranger every day.

CHAPTER 9

THE BEAUTY OF WORKING FOR YOURSELF IS THAT YOU CAN make your own hours and set your own schedule. The danger lies in turning into a total slacker. It's a slippery slope, I'll admit. One day, you decide to take it easy, go in late, blow off work, and next thing you know you're hooked on "Days of Our Lives" and eating ice cream out of the carton in your pajamas. Not that I've ever done that.

If anyone deserved a mental health day that Friday, it was me. I think we can all agree on that. And I wasn't even taking the whole day; I planned to go in at noon. I checked my e-mail, too, so I was sort of working. Luckily, only one e-mail needed a response and it was from Becca. I shuddered, remembering my dream, but a quick gulp of hot coffee jolted me back to reality. Her question was--did she have to give Joe the kids if he showed up drunk? He always went out Thursday nights with his friends and got wasted (she said), and she was afraid he'd still be drunk at pick-up time in the morning.

In retrospect, a degree in psychology or counseling would

have come in handy because I've had to learn this stuff on the job.

No, I wrote to Becca, *you definitely should not give Joe the children if he's drunk, BUT, there needs to be corroboration of his condition. Perhaps you should have an objective third party there to make that determination.* **It should not be your boyfriend, Charlie**. *Keep a log of anything that happens, and remember--Joe is the father of your children. I know it's tough, but the two of you have to find a way to parent together for your daughters' sake. Hopefully, the tension will subside after the divorce is final.*

Then, with the satisfaction of having done a full five minutes of work, I took my coffee and a book out to the patio so I could soak up some vitamin D rays and chill out. I must have dozed off at some point because I missed several calls. One was from my office and two were from Becca. So much for taking a few hours for myself. It was hard to decide which was more unpleasant, talking to Lisa, who might be crying, or Becca. It was a toss-up. As a compromise, I listened to Becca's voice mail. In her first message, she sounded annoyed. Joe hadn't shown to pick up the kids and he was already an hour late. But her second message was alarming. She sounded hysterical and said the police were at her door, could I please call her immediately. My heart started racing like it always does in a crisis, be it mine or anyone else's, so I pushed the call back button and waited nervously for her to pick up.

"Becca? It's Jamie. What's going on?"

"Jamie--the police are here, I can't talk right now." She sounded like she was crying.

"But, what's wrong? What happened?"

She sobbed. "It's Joe--he's dead!"

CHAPTER 10

I was shocked. What could've happened? Maybe a car accident or a violent crime, or a heart attack. Younger guys than Joe had dropped dead suddenly. That's why they call those early attacks 'widow makers'. Well, there wouldn't be any more bickering now, and there wouldn't be a divorce either. Those poor kids, Leah and Lainie, had been through so much already and now to lose their dad--it was tragic. There wasn't much I could do for that family, except leave them to their grief. Of course, if Becca needed anything, I'd try my best to help her.

It occurred to me that I hadn't finished preparing the order from our last hearing. Now I didn't need to, I'd be filing a dismissal instead. While I thought I'd seen everything before, this was a first for me, and I needed to think it through. Because Becca and Joe were still married at the time of his death and there was no prenuptial agreement, she would inherit all of their joint assets. Also, Joe had a life insurance policy with his wife and daughters as beneficiaries, so that would kick in. Finally, the girls were entitled to receive Social Security death benefits through their dad until they turned eighteen. Becca would be all set financially but, emotionally, she and her children had a long road ahead of them

Thinking about those young girls losing their dad was almost too much for me. Had my own dad been in a Cuban prison all these years? How could I not look for him now that I knew? And how terrible would it be to find him, yet be powerless to do anything? I wish my mother had told me about him sooner, but I understood her reasons. She knew I wouldn't let it go, that I wouldn't stop until I found him, and that it could only lead to heartache.

Maybe I could find the answer quickly and be done with it. If I knew my father was dead, at least I'd have closure, and I wouldn't have to wonder for the rest of my life. Who was I kidding? Nothing was ever easy, but at least I had some resources I could use. There were immigration attorneys I could call, I had Duke and Grace and all their connections, and I had the Internet. And I couldn't have lived in a better place. There were close to a million Cubans in South Florida, many of them with relatives in Cuba; surely, one of them could help me find my father.

As it turned out, I wouldn't be going to the office after all. I sat down at my computer with a steaming cup of coffee and a cat in my lap (yes, that's what I said) to begin making lists. It was time to start 'Project Dad'.

CHAPTER 11

I'M NOT EMBARRASSED TO TELL YOU I STARTED WITH Wikipedia. I wanted to get an overview of the political situation in Cuba and also the history since Castro took power. I was especially interested in a crackdown on Cuban dissidents in 2003 known as 'Black Spring', where the government had imprisoned seventy-five dissidents, including journalists and teachers, who were later adopted by Amnesty International as prisoners of conscience. The prisoners were eventually released and exiled to Spain, except for the ones that had died in prison. The website listed all of the prisoners, even the dead ones, but my father's name was not one of them.

I then looked for local organizations that could help me and the first one I found was 'The Cuban Liberty Council' in Miami, which was dedicated to promoting democracy in Cuba, and providing assistance to human rights and opposition groups in Cuba. That sounded promising. I kept looking and found an even better one: the 'Free Cuba Foundation', a non-profit/non-partisan organization working towards the establishment of an independent and democratic Cuba through non-violent means.

Their goals were to provide information on the situation inside of Cuba; provide a platform for human rights and democracy activists; and provide a means for the Internet community to engage in campaigns to free political prisoners, or improve their conditions. *They also provided a list of current political prisoners.* I was relieved to see my dad wasn't on that list either. That's not to say he couldn't be in prison for some other reason.

I knew it was a long shot, but I also ran my father's name through the SSDI (Social Security Death Index). He wouldn't have a Social Security number unless he was here legally or a citizen, and he wouldn't be on the SSDI unless he was a *dead* citizen, so I wasn't surprised when nothing came up. I even looked for him on Facebook. I was just deciding what to do next when my phone buzzed. It was a text from Becca. Finally! It had been over three hours since we'd talked.

Sorry I didn't call, she texted, *but I'm too upset to talk to anyone. The police think Joe died from an overdose. They won't know for sure until the autopsy. My girls haven't stopped crying. This is so awful...*

An overdose? I didn't see that coming. Joe didn't seem like the type--a drinker, yes, but not a druggie. And he hadn't struck me as suicidal, either. I know for a fact that he'd been looking forward to seeing his kids, and it seemed like he relished making Becca miserable.

I texted my condolences: *I'm so sorry, Becca. That's terrible news! Please let me know if I can help in any way. Don't hesitate to call me. All my best, Jamie*

As you can see, we family law attorneys have a skewed view of the world. How could we not? Everyone around us is acting crazy; lying all the time, fighting over stupid stuff, like microwave ovens, or toy trains they claim are family heirlooms. For the sake of our sanity, we have to walk away sometimes, go hang out with fun people. My go-to fun person was Grace, which was why I had her on speed dial.

"Is it happy hour yet?" I asked, when she answered the phone.

"It's five o'clock somewhere, I imagine. What are you drinking, a Cuba Libre?"

"A frozen rum runner is more like it."

"You got it, Amiga. Lucky it's Latin Night at Tekila's! See you in thirty."

I changed my clothes and went off to find my dose of sanity. The first place I planned to look was inside a tall glass, with a cherry on top.

CHAPTER 12

TEKILA'S IS A CASUAL BAR ON HOLLYWOOD BOULEVARD with a different theme every night. It's also a Mexican restaurant. Grace and I like to go there on Fridays for Latin Nights because we love the upbeat music and the quirky, fun people who dance to it. Not that we danced. I find walking without tripping enough of a challenge. Luckily, my name isn't Grace, so I don't have all that pressure.

I couldn't wait to unwind with my best friend and chat about our week, although I had no intention of talking about Becca. Her sad story was the reason I needed to get away in the first place.

The city of Hollywood is about thirty square miles altogether, so everything is close by. It only took me twenty minutes to get to Tekila's, even with rush hour traffic. Grace was already seated at the lacquered bar, dressed in her 'Casual Friday' clothes, which were still pretty chic, sipping a Margarita on the rocks, extra salt. I could see a frozen rum runner on the bar, waiting just for me. The glass hadn't even started to sweat.

"Wow!" I said, sliding onto the bar stool. "How did you get here so fast--jet pack?"

I scooched my drink closer and latched my mouth onto the straw. Instantly, sweet, tart, icy rum runner started gliding over my tongue, numbing and exciting it at the same time. I sighed with contentment. Funny how something so cold could make me feel so warm.

"I teleported," Grace said with a laugh. "Try to keep up, Jamie, will ya? Actually, I was around the corner picking up a transcript. I have a big trial coming up and my client is giving me an ulcer. At this rate, I'll have to start buying Rolaids by the case."

"Poor you!" I said, patting her arm with my cold, wet hand. She yanked her arm away and I laughed.

"He-ey!" She protested.

"I'm just trying to take your mind off your troubles," I said. "You're welcome." Then I went back to slurping my drink.

"I hope you get brain freeze," Grace said, matter-of-factly.

"Oh, I plan on it. But that won't stop me from ordering another one. How's your Margarita, lady? Does it meet your high standards?"

Grace snorted. "My standards are pretty low when it comes to Margaritas. All I need is a shot of tequila and some salt, and I'm happy."

"Speaking of low standards," I said, signaling Jan, our favorite bartender, for another round, "Did you finally dump that loser, Christopher, or did you take him back, *again?*"

Grace polished off her drink just as Jan placed a fresh one in front of her. Her timing was always impeccable.

"Sorry, I can't hear you, the music's too loud."

"Grace, seriously? You took him back? He totally mooches off you, he barely works, and he's not even nice. And now he's making *me* look like the bad guy. I ought to give you the spiel--

where's your self-respect, you deserve better, the whole thing, but I'm not gonna do it. You wouldn't listen, anyway."

"You're right."

"I know I am."

"I mean, you're right about me not listening." Grace said. "Look, I'm not crazy, Jamie. I see Christopher for who he is, but I still like him. He's funny and spontaneous and we have a good time together. I never said he was *Mr. Right*; he's just *Mr. Right Now*. Okay?"

"Alright, sorry. Just trying to look out for my BFF. I'll shut up now. Feel free to give me advice about my love life anytime," I said.

"I would, but..."

"But, what?"

"You don't have a love life." Grace gave me a sideways look.

"Oh, yeah, that's right. I don't." I sipped my second rum runner. Two is my limit, so I had to make this one last.

"What are we going to do about that?" Grace asked, tapping her foot to the music as she watched a couple salsa dancing across the room. They were good.

"One problem at a time, Grace," I said. "Right now, I'm looking for my dad, and I don't even know where to start. How am I supposed to obsess, if you keep trying to distract me?"

"Whoa, hold on a minute," she said, putting her drink down and giving me her full attention. "Yesterday, you were too freaked out to ask your aunt about your dad, and now you're devoting your life to finding him? Did I miss something?"

"Yeah, you did. I'll catch you up, but I'm going to need some tacos first. "

CHAPTER 13

"So, let me get this straight," Grace said, after we'd polished off two tacos each and an iced tea. "Your dad could be anywhere, including prison, or possibly dead, but wherever he is, he's definitely *not* looking for you, because he doesn't know there *is* a you?"

"Exactly--except you forgot the part about the political intrigue, the tragic love story, and the nagging question of whether I'm morally obligated to learn Spanish now. God knows I've tried, but the subjunctive tense makes me crazy. And the verb conjugations, Dios mio! There's a formal 'you,' an informal 'you,' a plural formal 'you,' and a plural informal 'you'-- like saying "you guys"--*but only if you happen to be in Spain.* It's way too complicated. Don't you think 'Spanglish' should be good enough? I mean, I'm only half-Cuban, you know?"

Grace laughed and shook her head. "You're losing it, girl! Seriously though, do you think it's a good idea to look for him? It's such a long shot and even if you found him, what then? Are you picturing a big family reunion?"

I knew she was trying to protect me. The truth was I'd only

begun to move past my mom's death and the last thing I needed was more heartache.

I sighed. "I promise not to get carried away. And no family reunions with matching t-shirts or anything like that. I'd just like to know what kind of person my dad is, or at least what happened to him. I know the odds of finding him are not good. It's like a "Where's Waldo" game that's the size of a small country. I have a better chance of winning the lottery."

"Well, I hope you bought a ticket, because it's up to $60 million." Grace smiled.

"You bet I did! And when I win, my friend, dinner is on me. *In Paris.*"

"You should book the Learjet now," she said, "Just to be safe."

As we were talking, Grace took her expensive, state-of -the art tablet out of her purse, placed it on the bar and started typing like a woman on a mission.

"What are you doing?" I asked, looking over her shoulder. "Don't tell me you're working right now, in the middle of Latin Night at Tekila's? No wonder you need so many Rolaids, you're a maniac."

Grace rolled her eyes. "Of course I'm not working, silly. I'm looking for Waldo. I have to warn you though, my Spanish is worse than yours, so, if we get stuck on a word, we'll have to use Google translator. Why don't you tell me what you've done so far?"

Ever since we'd met our second year at Nova Law, I could always count on Grace. Smarter than most and funny as hell, she was like a brilliant comet lighting up the long, black night that was law school. Okay, I'm exaggerating a little, but, believe me, law school was anything but fun.

With her black glasses and trendy clothes, Grace already looked the part of a lawyer, even back then, but underneath it all, she was such a goofball. I swear, nobody can make me laugh like Grace can, especially when she does funny voices. She can imitate almost anyone. I'll never forget the night Grace called our friend Suzie and pretended to be our cranky Torts professor, Maryellen Brennan. Grace had Suzie shaking in her shoes for a full fifteen minutes, while I sat next to her, cracking up. It wasn't until Grace told Suzie she should bake an apple torte for extra credit that she finally caught on.

Grace had another talent; one that all lawyers wish for, what I like to call 'the voice of reason.' The voice of reason is a voice that's calm, modulated, and as soothing as honey on a sore throat. Because of it, Grace always sounds like she's right.

In law school, you're taught that if the law isn't on your side, you should argue the facts, and if the facts aren't on your side, you should argue the law, but they teach you nothing about delivery, which can make all the difference. Sure, if you work at it, you can learn the mechanics of being an effective speaker: frequent eye contact; strong posture; controlling your pace; and using appropriate body language--like not flailing around and distracting people from what you're saying--but you'll never have the voice of reason, a voice so compelling that even if it recited the phone book to you, you'd have to listen. Think about it and you'll understand why James Earl Jones was the best person to be the voice of Darth Vader. Having the 'voice of reason' is why Grace sounds like she has all the answers, even when she doesn't.

∾

I told Grace everything I'd done, which wasn't much, to be honest, but considering I'd had to deal with Becca's crisis, it was still something. Then I asked her where she thought we should start.

"How about we Google 'how to find a lost relative in Cuba?'"

"Well, duh, why didn't I think of that?"

"You're too close to the problem," Grace said, kindly.

"Then I'm lucky I have you," I said. And I meant it.

CHAPTER 14

WE SPENT THE NEXT HOUR SITTING AT THE BAR AT Tekila's, brainstorming. I felt bad taking up seats for so long, but the crowd had thinned and Jan said she didn't mind. Yet another reason she's our favorite bartender.

Grace's idea about googling how to find a lost relative in Cuba turned up dozens of leads, mostly genealogy sites such as geneaology.com, FamilySearch, MyHeritage, and Cubagenweb.org, which was a how-to guide for genealogical research for Cuban people. While this information could prove useful eventually, I wasn't at that stage yet, since I knew nothing about my father or his (and my) relatives in Cuba, not to mention that he had a fairly common surname and I didn't know his place of birth. The only thing I knew for sure was his age. In her letter, my mom had mentioned that they'd met when they were both twenty. Since she would've been fifty-five this year, he'd be fifty-five as well.

In our Internet treasure hunt, we also discovered "Cuba Google" and "Cuba blogs," which looked promising, but since neither of us spoke Spanish, we decided to leave those for last, maybe find someone to translate for us. Grace liked the blog idea. She was convinced that anyone as politically active as my dad would've left an Internet footprint, specifically a blog, but I wasn't so sure. Maybe being arrested and deported and losing the woman he loved had left him feeling defeated. And, if it turned out he was in prison, he sure couldn't maintain a blog from his cell.

At the end of the night, it looked like one of our best leads was the Cuban American National Foundation in Miami, which provided information to people about their relatives in Cuba, or provided contacts to help them find that information. The other promising lead was the Cuban Consulate in Washington, D.C. Grace had a friend who worked for the state department in D.C. whom she planned to call and ask for advice. I said I would contact the Cuban America National Foundation, as well as the other Miami groups I'd found while doing my own research.

"It's a good start," Grace said, as she slipped her tablet back in her purse. "Do you think we should ask Duke for help? He did offer."

"I would, but I can't think of anything for him to do right now. We should wait until we really need him, you know, for the cloak and dagger stuff."

"Cloak and dagger--listen to you! I told you that watching so much TV would fry your brain, Jamie, and now it's happened. Such a shame."

"Don't be jealous, Grace. One day, you'll have the time to enjoy 'quality couch time' like I do, with a remote control in one hand and an iced latte in the other. I can see it now--you'll dance in the aisles with Ellen DeGeneres, learn 'what not to wear' and become a gourmet chef, all without leaving the sofa. What a life!"

"'Thanks, but I'd rather drink a Margarita with my friend and watch people salsa dance *in the real world*," Grace said.

"Or, you could come over; we'll make Margaritas and watch 'Dancing with the Stars' on my couch. It's su-per comfortable."

"You're a nut, you know that?" She smiled. "I think I'll call it a night so you can go catch up on your shows."

I laughed as I slipped into one of our old jokes, borrowed from the great George Burns. "Say good night, Gracie."

"Good night, Gracie," she said, and then she yawned, which wasn't part of the routine, but still a nice touch.

CHAPTER 15

I spent the weekend doing boring weekend stuff--laundry, groceries, paying bills, cleaning house and, of course, catching up on my shows. I always like to start my week with a full tank of gas, a full fridge and money in my wallet; otherwise, I feel like I'm behind before I even get started. Having clean clothes to wear is also high on the list. It's strange, but I find working every day hard to get used to, although I did it for ten years before my mom died. It seems that once you stop punching a clock, you immediately forget how to do it; and then, you don't even remember what the clock looks like.

Given that I'm fairly obsessive, you might think I showed remarkable restraint by not spending the weekend online looking for my father, but the truth is my brain was on overload. If I didn't have some downtime to absorb all that new information, my head would explode. Besides being obsessive, I'm also hyperbolic, which sounds like a disease, but isn't.

I was glad I hadn't planned to have Sunday dinner with Aunt Peg and Adam. I didn't feel like talking about my mom, my dad, family secrets, or anything that came under those headings. Instead, I invited my next-door neighbors, Sandy and Mike, over for Indian take-out and a glass of wine. It was fun and relaxing and just what the doctor ordered--if you could get a doctor to write you a prescription for Curry, Pinot Grigio, and an evening in the company of nice people.

By Monday morning, I was refreshed and ready to tackle the world, or at least ready to tackle my in-box. I was in such a good mood, I could've even handled Lisa's crying, but I hoped I wouldn't have to. As a precaution, and to spread the good cheer around, I stopped at Einstein's on my way to work to pick up a dozen bagels for the office, including cinnamon-raisin, Lisa's favorite.

After I settled in at my desk with a second cup of coffee, I e-mailed Becca to ask about Joe's funeral arrangements as I felt obligated to pay my respects. It occurred to me that Joe's parents might be the ones making the arrangements, considering the bitter divorce proceedings, but Becca would still have the information.

I worked non-stop until lunchtime and managed to jam out quite a bit of paperwork, if I do say so myself. I wish I were a steady worker, but, unfortunately, I only have two speeds: full-speed ahead and dead-stop. Happily, it was a full-speed kind of day. I was mulling over whether to get a sub or a salad from the delivery place across the street when my cell phone rang. I normally don't answer it at lunchtime as a way to establish boundaries for my clients. Just because they have my cell number (which is more for my convenience than for theirs), doesn't mean that I'm on call for them 24/7. But I saw it was Becca, so I decided to pick up.

"Hey, Becca, I've been thinking about you. How are you holding up, sweetie?"

"I'm not, Jamie, not at all." Her voice sounded ragged, like she'd been crying all weekend.

"I can only imagine. You must be overwhelmed, how can I help?"

"I'm calling because I don't know what to do," she wailed. "The state attorney's office called and asked me to come in for questioning. Why would they do that? What do they want from me? Why is this happening? I can't take it anymore!"

I could hear her hysteria escalating and I knew I had to talk her down off the ledge, figuratively speaking. At least I hoped it was figurative. You never know a person's limits; and sometimes, you don't even know your own.

"It's okay, Becca. It's probably just a routine thing. Listen, I know someone at the state attorney's office, how about I call him for you and see what I can find out?"

She paused and then in a voice as small as a little girl's, she said, "Yes, please...and will you call me back?"

"I promise. But don't sit by the phone waiting because sometimes it takes a while for him to return the call. Why don't you go make yourself some tea, or lie down and relax for a bit? Okay?"

"I'll try," she said, not very convincingly.

After we hung up, I dialed the direct line of Nick Dimitropoulos, State Attorney, rising star, son of a senator, and my arch-enemy. If you look up the word 'arch' in the dictionary, you'll find that it refers to a person with an amused feeling of being superior to or knowing more than other people. Next to that definition, you'll see a picture of Nick D. Oh wait, that's just in my dictionary.

I come by my feelings for Nick, honestly. He's the one who went after my disabled cousin, Adam, a year earlier and tried to pin a murder on him using only circumstantial evidence and a truckload of political ambition. We finally reached a truce after I convinced him to focus on the real killer. He ended up looking like a hero, with his picture in the paper and all the accolades to go with it, so he owed me one, and he knew it. Politicians always keep score of favors, even wannabe politicians. Especially wannabe politicians.

"Nick Dimitropoulos."

Hearing his voice, I pictured him at his desk with his chiseled jaw and perfectly trimmed nails. He'd be wearing the latest from Armani, shiny wingtip shoes (with or without tassels) and not one hair out of place. His desk would be neatly organized and equipped with the best technology money can buy.

"Jamie Quinn here, how's it going, Nick?"

"Hello Quinn--I didn't expect to hear from you so soon."

I laughed. "So soon? It's been a year since I helped you get your picture in the paper."

"For your information, Quinn, my picture is in the paper all the time. And for all the right reasons."

"I don't doubt that for a minute, Nick..." I hesitated, unsure exactly how to proceed.

"So, Quinn, what can I do for you? Are you looking for a reference?"

I burst out laughing. "You're kidding, right?"

"Of course I am. What's up?"

"Well, I have a client--"

"Another cousin of yours?"

"Funny one, Nick. And no, not a cousin. One of my clients received a call from your office this morning asking her to come in. I'd like to know why."

"What's her name?"

"Becca Solomon."

"I'm familiar with that case."

"It's a case? Why is it a case? Her husband was found dead last Friday, but she knew nothing about it. She was waiting for him to pick up the kids."

There was a pause as Nick seemed to consider what information he was willing to share.

"Quinn, I shouldn't be telling you this, but Joe Solomon died from a combination of alcohol and sleeping pills."

"I don't follow. Why shouldn't you tell me?"

"Because they were your client's sleeping pills."

CHAPTER 16

"THERE MUST BE AN EXPLANATION--"I SPUTTERED.

"There's always an explanation," Nick said. "But it may not be the one you want to hear."

"I'll keep an open mind, thank you, and I'd advise you to do the same. Remember the last time you went for the low-hanging fruit? *You had the wrong guy.* Lawsuits have been filed for less, Nick. I'm just sayin'."

"I'm not worried, Quinn."

He was hard to rattle, I'll give him that.

"I assume your client will be calling us to set an appointment?" he asked with his usual smugness. "Or do you want to set it now?"

"I'll call you back," I said, trying to buy some time.

I was amazed to find myself, once again, embroiled in a criminal case. How does this keep happening to me? My business card says 'Family Law Attorney' on it, plain as day. And poor Becca! Before I called her and pushed her right off that ledge she was teetering on, I needed to get some advice so I could guide her in the right direction. She seemed so helpless, so broken. I knew just who to call: Susan Doyle, public defender extraordinaire. Susan had been invaluable when my cousin, Adam, was accused of murder; without her, I don't know what would've happened to Adam. Nothing good, that's for sure.

When I called the public defender's office and asked for Susan Doyle, I was told she no longer worked there, that she'd gone into private practice. I don't know why I was surprised. My life had changed in the past year; it was silly of me to think that other people were standing still. The receptionist was nice enough to give me Susan's number. To my relief, she hadn't moved away; her practice was in downtown Hollywood, three blocks from the courthouse.

I left a message for Susan and she called me right back. After we chatted a little and she'd asked about Adam, I launched into my reason for calling.

"Susan, I have a situation, well, my client does, and I was hoping you could help and possibly represent her, if necessary. This woman can afford private counsel and I would advise her to hire you."

"Of course, Jamie, anything I can do. What's going on?"

I told her about my conversation with 'Slick Nick,' (as Susan liked to call him), and the rundown of Becca and Joe's divorce litigation, in all its nastiness.

"That's quite a story," Susan said. "You've known Becca a while, what's your take on her? Do you think she had anything to do with his death?"

I thought for a minute. "I don't think she's capable of it. She is genuinely falling apart and she seemed as shocked as the rest of us when Joe turned up dead. She was actually waiting for him to pick up the kids when she found out."

Then Susan asked a question that caught me off guard. "Did she ever threaten his life?"

I gasped as I remembered our last court hearing. "I'm afraid she did. She told him that if he tried to take the kids away from her, she would kill him!"

Susan was unfazed. She'd been a public defender a long time and she'd heard much worse, I was sure of it.

"Did anyone else hear her threaten him?"

"Yeah, come to think of it. Judge Marcus' bailiff, Harold, was there and he said he would call security if they didn't calm down."

"Well, that's not going to help," Susan said, "but at least we know it's out there. Information is power, I always say. You mentioned that Joe moved out of the marital home a month ago, did Becca have a key to his residence?"

I knew why she was asking. If Becca had a motive to kill Joe, and Nick would certainly think she had one, did she also have the opportunity?"

"No, Becca definitely didn't have access to his house. They wouldn't give each other the time of day, let alone exchange keys. Becca even had the locks changed on the marital home so Joe couldn't come in."

My stomach was growling, reminding me that I never did get around to ordering lunch. I'm not usually a person who forgets to eat, I can assure you.

Susan paused, and then asked, "Suicide? Accident?"

"No to suicide. Accident is a possibility." I was searching my desk drawers for crackers or anything to eat. All I found were a couple of loose Chiclets. I shoved them in my mouth.

"One more question, do either of them have a lover? That tends to change the dynamics."

I almost swallowed my Chiclets. I'd forgotten about Becca's boyfriend!

"Yes! Becca has a boyfriend; he used to be a friend of Joe's, but not anymore, of course. His name is Charlie Santoro. I met him a couple of times and he seemed like a mellow guy. He wasn't adding fuel to the fire, if that's what you're asking."

Susan didn't pull any punches. "Do you think he could be a suspect?

I thought about it. "No idea. I guess anything's possible. I've been fooled by people before. The mantra of the family law attorney is 'everybody lies.'"

Susan laughed. "Don't forget you're talking to a criminal attorney. Our clients tell so many lies, they wouldn't know the truth if it bit them in the ass."

I chuckled along with her.

"Okay," Susan said, in her no-nonsense way, "here's what you do. Set up the meeting with the state attorney's office and go in with Becca. Don't let her answer any questions except for her name and address. After that, plead the fifth on the grounds that she might incriminate herself. We'll make the state attorney do the work. If charges are filed, then I'll meet with Becca and she can formally retain me."

"What else can I do to help?"

"Do you still have the number for that strange PI? I think we need his services. What was his name?"

"Duke Broussard. Yeah, he's strange alright."

CHAPTER 17

Before we wrapped up our conversation, Susan explained what she needed from Duke. Since the burden of proof in a criminal case is 'beyond a reasonable doubt', Duke's role would be to create that doubt, to dig up evidence that pointed *away* from Becca, in the event she was charged with a crime. Susan recommended that Becca hire Duke right away because the sooner he could clear her name, the better.

I was dreading making that call to Becca. Don't get me wrong, as a family law attorney, I've delivered plenty of bad news to clients before, but it's never easy. And how exactly do you tell someone they're a murder suspect? Is there a class on that? A website? The only consolation was that Becca would be hearing it from me, and not Nick.

I wandered into the small kitchen of our office in search of food. My hunger was starting to crowd out all other thoughts; also, I was getting a headache. To my surprise, the Einstein's box I'd brought that morning still had three bagels in it. And there was half a tub of cream cheese, too. Oh happy day! I didn't bother to look for a knife; I just ripped a pumpernickel bagel in half and used it to scoop up the cream cheese and shovel it into my mouth. I'm sure I looked like a wild beast tearing into an antelope, but I didn't care. I was *that* hungry. Besides, as a vegetarian, I would never eat antelope.

With my stomach stuffed full of bagels, my reasoning power returned and it told me to call Duke first; that way I could present Becca with a solution at the same time I told her the problem. Also, I needed to know if Duke was available (as if he could resist a damsel in distress and a whodunit all rolled into one); also, what he would charge for his services; and what his plan of attack would be. I was glad I could finally offer Duke a paying job and I was equally glad that I could put off calling Becca.

When he picked up the phone, I could hear the bar crowd in the background. He had to be hanging out at "The Big Easy;" Duke practically lived there.

"Well, if it isn't Ms. Esquire, herself." Duke said. "I knew you couldn't stay away. It's that Broussard charm--it gets under your skin."

"You know, I *have* been feeling itchy lately. I thought it was a rash, but it must've been that old Broussard charm."

Duke laughed. "How's it going, Darlin'? Ready to start looking for your daddy again? I have some ideas."

For a second, I forgot that Duke wasn't up to speed on my dad project. There wasn't much to tell, anyway, but today was not the day.

"You've been great for helping me with that, Duke, and I really appreciate it, but I put the project on hold for now. I have a divorce case that's turned into a murder investigation and I need the services of a good PI. You in?"

"Nah. Not unless you need the services of a *great* PI. I can't be lowering my standards like that, you know. It would ruin my reputation."

I laughed. "Well, I wouldn't want that on my conscience. This would be a paid gig, just so you know."

"Well, why didn't you say so? I'll lower my standards if the price is right. Does $75 an hour sound fair? I'll need a retainer up front, maybe $500. Does that work?"

It sounded like Duke could use the money.

"I'm sure that will be fine," I said, and then I told him what was going on with Becca.

"Wow!" he said when I'd finished. "That's a juicy one. When do we get started?"

"Right after I tell Becca she's a suspect in her husband's murder."

CHAPTER 18

I COULDN'T PUT IT OFF ANY LONGER; SO I DIALED BECCA'S number. To my surprise, a man answered.

"Becca's phone."

"Hi, this is Jamie Quinn. May I please speak with Becca?"

"Oh, hey Jamie, it's Charlie. Becca's sleeping, but she said to wake her if you called. I don't think she slept all weekend. Man, this has been rough on her."

"I bet it has. You know what, Charlie? Don't wake her, I can call back later. But I wanted to ask you something--had you seen Joe recently?"

"I used to see him around town and stuff. I always said 'hi'--I mean, I felt bad for the guy--but he just ignored me."

"Did you two ever argue? Was he nasty to you?" I asked.

Charlie paused before answering. "Yeah, when he first found out I was seeing Becca, he called and chewed my ass out, said I was a bastard, a son of a bitch, and a few other things. But then he quit talking to me altogether."

After we'd hung up, I wondered how Charlie and Joe had become friends to begin with. Charlie was low-key, good looking in a scruffy way, like a surfer dude, or a guy playing Frisbee with his dog on the beach. Joe, on the other hand, was ambitious, high energy, loud. He liked nice clothes and expensive cars and enjoyed being the center of attention. Having built a tech business which he later sold for a million dollars, Joe liked to think he was the next Steve Jobs. As far as friends go, those two seemed completely mismatched. In any case, I couldn't picture Charlie killing anyone. *Too much bad karma and stuff, man.*

It was 3:00, but I was done with work for the day. God bless self-employment! I felt like I'd accomplished a lot, or at least enough, and I needed to clear my head. I decided a little exercise with some nature thrown in was just the ticket, so I headed over to T.Y. Park for a long walk. I always keep exercise clothes and sneakers in my car, in case the mood strikes me, but, since it rarely does, the clothes were fresh and clean. If they'd ever been sweated in at all...

Topeekeegee Yugnee Park, T.Y. for short, lives up to its name, which means "meeting or gathering place" in the Seminole language. At 138 acres, it's an urban park right in the middle of town with a two mile paved loop shared convivially by walkers, joggers, skaters, bikers, and moms lulling their babies to sleep in strollers. Even at mid-afternoon on a Monday, it was brimming with people. The park has a lot to offer: bikes and boats for rent, campgrounds and playgrounds, basketball, volleyball and tennis, and over a dozen picnic shelters for parties and barbecues. But the best thing about T.Y. is Castaway Island, a large water park with slides, pools and a beach.

Back in high school, I used to work at the concession stand during the summer and, despite the fact that it was broiling hot, swarming with kids, and crazy busy all the time, it was the most fun I ever had. But then, I wasn't a lifeguard, which was an exhausting, high pressure job. It's amazing how many parents think they don't have to watch their kids around water just because there's a lifeguard on duty. For about $10/hour, our lifeguards saved at least five kids a day from drowning.

The fun came after we closed the park at 5:00. That's when the staff could play on the slides and swim in the pools. It was a blast! We enjoyed it even more because we had to wait for it all day. It shouldn't surprise you to hear that a few romances got their start during our daily water games.

As I walked the loop, I took a detour over to Castaway Island. Hearing kids squealing and laughing transported me back to those amazing summers. I was standing there, daydreaming, when someone tapped me on the shoulder.

"Jamie? I can't believe it, you look exactly the same! Don't you recognize me?"

"Um, sorry, I'm not sure I do," I said to the gorgeous guy standing next to me. He was easily a foot taller than me, with smiling brown eyes, sun bleached hair, and so tan he must've spent a lot of time outdoors. I studied his face for clues; this was really embarrassing. And then I almost keeled over.

"Kip? Oh my God! It's really you!" My voice was squeaking I was so happy to see him. "Sorry I didn't recognize you, I mean--you've changed so much. When did you get so tall?" I couldn't stop smiling. Or babbling. Kip and I were one of those waterpark romances I told you about. I was crazy about him back then, and I think he felt the same way about me, but when he went away to college, we drifted apart. I still thought about him sometimes, especially when I drove past the park.

Before I could say another word, he gave me a big hug and scooped me off the ground. And then he laughed and put me back down.

"Yeah, I had a bit of a growth spurt in college, you know?"

He grinned. "It's fantastic to see you, Jamie! How have you been? What are you doing with yourself?"

"Let's see, I got a degree in English literature, realized I had no marketable skills, and then went to law school. Now, I'm a family law attorney here in Hollywood. What about you?" I couldn't stop staring at him.

"I took a long and torturous route, myself. I came out of school with an MBA, went straight into the corporate world and hated it. Did a 180, went back to school, and ended up with a job I love, working outdoors where I can worship nature in all her glory." He stopped to kick a soccer ball back to a little boy, who quickly resumed his game.

"That's great!" I said. "You always were her biggest fan. I can't believe we ran into each other here, of all places. What are the chances?"

He laughed. "I'd say the chances are excellent."

"What do you mean?"

"After I got my degree in park management and forestry, I worked for the state park system in California until they had budget cuts and I lost my job. A position opened up here and I applied for it. As of a week ago, I'm the new Director of the Parks Department. So, I work here."

"You work in this park?" I asked, trying to keep the excitement out of my voice. I was a grown-up now; I had to keep reminding myself.

"Actually, I'm in charge of all of the parks. I'm visiting each one to make assessments and I thought I'd start with my favorite one. But, tell me more about you, are you married? Have any kids?"

"Nope, how about you?" He had to be married. And he probably had a dozen gorgeous kids that looked just like him.

"I was engaged once for a few months, but it didn't work out. No kids either."

Someone, wake me up! On second thought, please don't.

We just stood there, smiling at each other until Kip took my hand and said, "I have to get back to work, but I'd love to catch up some more."

"I'd love that."

"Do you like horseback riding, by any chance? I have to go to Tradewinds Park next Saturday, and they have stables and horse trails."

"The last horse I was on was a pony when I was five, but that sounds like fun. If you don't mind riding with a novice."

"No worries, I'll teach you. How about we meet there at one o'clock?"

"Perfect! I'm looking forward to it, Kip."

"Me too. See you then, Jamie!" Another quick hug and he was gone.

I was dazed by my good fortune--that was Kip! We have a date! So what, if I don't know how to ride a horse, Kip's going to teach me. How was I going to make it to Saturday? I wondered. I knew that going on one date didn't necessarily mean anything, but I was happy right then, and nothing could change that.

I walked back to the parking lot and found my car. As I opened the door, I heard a frantic buzzing under the seat. I'd missed three calls from Becca.

CHAPTER 19

"Becca? It's Jamie. Sorry I missed you."

"It's okay," she said in a flat, monotone voice.

"I spoke with the state attorney. I'll tell you what he said in a minute, but first, I need to ask you a few questions."

"Alright."

I wondered if she was medicated, she sounded so robotic. She couldn't have sounded less interested if we were talking about the weather, or the Kardashians. I was still at the park, sitting in my car with the windows open. If I had to do something this unpleasant, I could at least enjoy the scenery.

"Do you feel okay?" I asked. "Would you rather I called back later?"

"It's fine," she intoned.

"Okay then, when is the last time you saw Joe?"

"In the courtroom."

"Did you talk to him after that?"

"No."

"On a different topic, do you have a prescription for sleeping pills, Becca?"

"Yes, Ambien."

She still sounded dull, almost bored.

"Do you take them often?"

"When I need to."

"Did Joe ever take your sleeping pills?"

"Yes."

Okay, now, we were getting somewhere.

"How many times did he do that?"

"Not sure. A few times."

"Do you know how he would've gotten any of your pills after he moved out?"

"Not really."

"Could he have taken some with him when he moved out?"

"I guess."

"Is Charlie there? Would you mind putting him on the phone for a minute?"

I heard her hand him the phone.

"Hi Jamie," he said.

"Hi Charlie, is Becca okay? She doesn't sound right. I need to talk to her about some important things and I don't know if she is, well, paying attention."

"Yeah, when she gets too stressed, she sort of shuts down. She'll be back to normal soon."

I remembered that she acted the same way in the courthouse lobby, after her hearing. Maybe this would make my job easier.

"Please ask Becca if she gives me permission to talk to you about her situation."

I heard him ask and I heard her agree.

"Okay, Charlie, here's the deal, the state attorney's office wants to question Becca as part of their investigation into Joe's death. We need to make an appointment and I plan to go with her. They'll probably want to talk to you at some point, too, I'm guessing. I'm sorry, but I wouldn't be able to represent both you and Becca, due to a potential conflict of interest, but I would strongly suggest you go with an attorney. If you can't afford one, you can ask them to appoint one for you from the public defender's office."

"It's cool, I understand. I'll tell her everything you said," he said, in his usual placid tone.

"Have her call me?"

"Sure."

It occurred to me after I'd hung up that Charlie hadn't shown any more emotion than Becca, even after I told him the state attorney might question him about his girlfriend's dead husband. There was something strange about Charlie; I just couldn't put my finger on it.

CHAPTER 20

I HADN'T TOLD CHARLIE ABOUT SUSAN DOYLE's suggestion to hire a PI. Like I said, there was a potential conflict of interest there, and my obligation was to Becca-- especially if the PI, a/k/a Duke, thought Charlie was worth investigating. I decided to take the easy way out this time and e-mail Becca, since I hadn't had much luck talking with her on the phone. Lord knows, I'd tried.

I'd been home for a while and had just finished feeding myself and the cat. My dinner was a frozen pizza, his was some smelly wet mix of who knows what that cats seem to enjoy. We were both happy with our selection.

After lounging around a bit, reading the news online, and playing "Words with Friends" with Grace, (since when is 'suqs' a word?), I dashed off an e-mail to Becca

Hi Becca, I called a friend of mine for advice on your situation and she believes it would be in your best interest to hire a private investigator to look into Joe's death. I agree with her. I have a PI I use who is very good and reasonably priced. He charges

*$75/hour and requires a $500.00 retainer up front. You have money left in my trust account from your divorce case which you could use to retain him, but you'd need to sign his retainer agreement. **Do you want to do that?** Also, we need to make an appointment with the state attorney. Please tell me when you're available and I'll make the appointment.*

Within two minutes, I had a reply.

Hi Jamie, you can go ahead and hire the PI. Can you email me his agreement? I can go with you to the state attny any morning after 8:30, but I can't go in the afternoon because I need to pick up the girls from school. Thanks for everything you're doing for me. Sorry I'm such a mess.

At least she sounded normal again. I quickly texted Duke that we were going ahead, and asked him to e-mail me his contract for Becca to sign. He texted me right back.

Hey Lawyer Lady-what are you going on about? What contract?
You know, like when people hire you? I texted back.
I operate on a handshake, Darlin'. No complaints as long as I get the job done.
Maybe because you get your business from your fellow barflies. And through that billboard your ex bought telling the world what she thought of you.
That did get me some business, didn't it? It served her right, after all the alimony I paid that woman.
Well, you're going to need a contract this time, Bucko. Or I'm not releasing the money from my trust account. And I can't draft it for you because Becca's my client. How about if I send you my retainer agreement & you can cut and paste from that.
You know, for a lawyer, you're not half bad.

Right back at ya.

After I e-mailed Duke my standard retainer agreement, I poured myself a glass of wine and kicked back on the sofa. To my dismay, there was a spring poking me in the behind that hadn't been there before. Time for a new sofa! I mean, how could I enjoy 'quality couch time' if I didn't have a couch that was up to the task? I hadn't changed anything since I'd inherited the house almost two years ago, so maybe it was time, but I sure didn't need another project right now. In the meantime, I'd just have to slide down to the poke-free end of the sofa where I could zone out, sip my wine and wonder who killed Joe Solomon.

CHAPTER 21

A BAGEL CAN BUY YOU A LOT OF GOOD WILL. I FOUND THAT out on Tuesday when I asked Lisa to do me a favor by calling the state attorney's office. She not only did it immediately, she did it with a smile. Who knew that's all it would take?

After Lisa set it up, I e-mailed Becca to tell her the appointment was Thursday morning and to ask her to come in a half-hour early to prepare. She e-mailed me right back to confirm. She also thanked me for offering to attend Joe's funeral, which would be Saturday morning, but asked me not to go. It would be hard enough on Joe's parents that she would be there; it would be that much worse if her divorce attorney were there.

I hadn't thought it through, but she was right; of course I shouldn't be there. It's not like I wanted to go in the first place (nobody *wants* to go to a funeral), and now that I had a date with Kip on Saturday, it had all worked out perfectly.

Skimming through the rest of my e-mails, I saw that Duke had sent over 'his' retainer agreement for Becca. I read it through to see if it made sense and it was alright, not bad at all, so I forwarded it to Becca for her signature. Once she sent it back, I'd be able to pay Duke from the trust account and he could get started on her case.

I was slogging through the work on my desk when I heard a familiar buzz. It was a text from Grace asking if I wanted to meet for lunch. She had depositions scheduled all afternoon in Hollywood around the corner from my office. Also, she had some news for me, she said. Well, I had some news for her, too. We agreed to meet at Exotic Bites on Harrison Street, since we were both in the mood for falafel, and theirs was the best in town. So, it was a no-brainer: hummus at high noon on Harrison Street.

I was studying the hookahs at the hookah bar when Grace walked into the restaurant.

"Hello, my favorite corporate lawyer," I said, giving her a peck on the cheek. "You look fabulous, as always."

"What, this old thing?" She said with a laugh, pointing at her red Anne Klein suit that fit her to perfection. We can't all wear Anne Klein the way Grace can, but then, some of us would rather be wearing sweat pants, anyway. Like me, for instance.

As we sat down, I suddenly remembered something.

"Hey, are you going to be okay eating here? Or will you have to chew on Rolaids the rest of the day?"

"I'll be fine," she said. "I only need Rolaids when I'm dealing with that client who stresses me out. Food doesn't bother me, just him. I can't wait for that case to be over."

"I bet!" I understood about difficult clients. I had a few, myself.

We were the first of the lunch crowd to arrive, so we got our food fast. Falafel sandwiches are really messy and it was all we could do not to drop food on our clothes.

It wasn't until we were sipping coffee and splitting a baklava that Grace said, "Don't you want to know what my news is? It's not like you to be so patient. Are you feeling okay?"

I laughed. "Maybe I'm turning over a new leaf. People can change, you know."

"Not a chance. What's really going on?" Grace looked skeptical, but I kept my face blank as long as I could.

"Okay," I said, "I'll tell you. I have a date on Saturday."

"No way! Who's the lucky guy? Do I know him? You've been holding out on me, Jamie. Spill it!"

"Well, he's wonderful and totally adorable, and we're going horseback riding at Tradewinds Park."

Grace looked exasperated. "But how did you meet? What's his name? Wait--did you say horseback riding? Is that a good idea? I mean, you're not the most athletic person. No offense."

"Don't worry. Kip said he'd teach me," I said, waiting for Grace's reaction.

"Kip? As in Kip Simons your high school boyfriend? How in the world--?"

"I love it when you're speechless!" I said, laughing. "I actually ran into him at T.Y. Park, he's the new Director of the Parks department! Isn't that fantastic? I didn't recognize him at first, but we hit it off again right away."

Grace shook her head. "Incredible! But, what were you doing in T.Y. Park? Trying to get your old job back?"

"Very funny! I was exercising, I'll have you know. I do that occasionally."

"I am so happy for you, Jamie, I really am. And it's about time. Now I get to give you advice about your love life! I can't wait."

"Hang on, Grace. I don't have a love life yet. But go ahead, give me some advice."

"Okay, I have three words for you."

"'Take it slow?'" I guessed.

"No," she laughed, "Wear--a--helmet. I can just see you falling off the horse!"

"Yeah," I said, "Me too."

CHAPTER 22

"Okay, Jamie, that was a bombshell, but I can top it. Do you want to hear my news now?" Grace asked, leaning forward. She was very excited.

I nodded. I couldn't imagine what she was going to say, but I suddenly had butterflies in my stomach.

"I spoke to my friend at the D.C. Consulate about your dad," Grace said. "And he did some research for me."

I sat there, twisting my napkin, waiting for the news.

Grace reached over the table and squeezed my hands. "He's alive, Jamie!"

"Oh, my God, my dad's alive!" I was so overwhelmed, I thought I would faint, or throw up. My hands were shaking like crazy and tears were streaming down my face.

"Here's what happened, you're not going to believe this story! Your dad escaped from a Cuban jail in 2005 and swam to a U.S. naval base where he waited four years for political asylum. When it wasn't granted, they flew him to Nicaragua with fifteen other Cubans. My friend called someone he knows at the Nicaraguan Consulate who pulled some strings and found out your dad is still in Nicaragua. They are trying to get an address for you, Jamie; you just need to hang in there. Isn't that totally freaking awesome?!"

I practically jumped across the table and pulled Grace into a hug. We were laughing and crying and carrying on like maniacs. A lifetime of grief over my lost father seemed to melt away in an instant. I felt weightless, like a dancer in mid-air, or a balloon about to float away.

A woman at another table caught my eye and grinned, our joy was contagious. She turned around to the waitress taking her order and joked, "I'll have what they're having."

CHAPTER 23

My euphoria lasted all day and I wanted to share the news with someone. I thought about calling Aunt Peg, but then decided not to. She's so pragmatic, I was afraid she'd start asking tough questions like, how did I know my dad wanted to hear from me? Not everyone would welcome the news of a grown daughter from a past life. And, did I really want to learn the details of his tragic life? And what if he needed help that I couldn't give him? Wouldn't I feel worse than I did before? So, I didn't call her. I called Duke instead.

"Hey Duke, how's it going?"

"Couldn't be better, Darlin'. The world is spinning, the sun is shining and I have a hot date tonight. How about you? We ready to roll with my new favorite client?"

"Yes, we are. I'll e-mail you a summary and the contact info for Becca. I also have some news."

"Hope its good news. I wouldn't want you to kill my buzz."

"Be serious, Duke, nothing could kill your buzz!" I laughed.

"You got me there." He chuckled.

"So, here's my big news, I'm close to finding my dad! He's living in Nicaragua and Grace is working on getting his address for me. Isn't that great?"

"That's terrific, Jamie. I'm very happy for you," Duke said, dully.

"Then why don't you sound happy?" I asked, puzzled by his reaction.

"I guess you figured Grace could help you more than I could. No problem."

Poor Duke! I'd hurt his pride. I can be so dense, sometimes. How was I going to fix this?

"But it was your lead that made it happen, Duke. Grace took a chance and called a friend at the Cuban Consulate who was able to track down my dad--but only because you did the groundwork. That's why I'm calling you first."

"You really called me first?" I could hear his smile through the phone.

"Of course! I couldn't have found him without you. You're the best!"

"Yeah, I am, aren't I? Keep me posted on that. I want to be the first one to shake the old man's hand."

"You just want to hit him up for Cuban cigars."

"What's wrong with that?" He laughed. "Congrats, Jamie, I mean it. Now, how about a little background on Becca Solomon?"

I filled him in on everything, including the upcoming appointment with the State Attorney, but I asked him to hold off talking to Becca until after the funeral on Saturday, and he agreed.

After our call, I e-mailed Duke the signed retainer from Becca, as well as other information he needed. It didn't take long, since I'd already given him a summary over the phone.

When I was through, I pulled out the file for one of my other cases because, believe it or not, I had more than one client, and there was a hearing scheduled for the next day that I needed to prepare for. It was a relief to focus on something mundane and forget about Becca Solomon for a while.

CHAPTER 24

WEDNESDAY PASSED UNEVENTFULLY. MY HEARING WENT smoothly, my client was granted the relief he was seeking and I felt good about being a family lawyer. Hey, it happens. And then Thursday arrived and it was time to meet with Becca. I was relieved to see she was dressed appropriately in a charcoal gray suit and that she seemed to be sharp and with it. I couldn't have handled it if she turned zombie on me again.

"How are you feeling, Becca?" I asked, once we were seated at my small conference table.

"I'm okay. I want to get this over with." She was bouncing her leg under the table. Her nervous energy had to escape somehow.

"Me too." I smiled, reassuringly. "You need to prepare yourself for this, mentally, because it's going to be tough, I won't lie to you. The state attorney will ask you lots of questions--about Joe, your relationship, your sleeping pill prescription, anything he can think of. And he's going to try to rattle you into an emotional outburst."

She looked panicky. "What do I do?"

"That's the easy part. After you provide your name and address, you're not going to answer any questions. Instead, you will say this: "I refuse to answer that on the grounds that it might incriminate me."

"What?? Are you kidding? That makes me sound like a criminal and I didn't do anything wrong! Whose side are you on, Jamie?"

"Calm down, Becca. I'm on your side and nobody said you did anything wrong. I spoke with an excellent criminal defense attorney, Susan Doyle, and she advised me to proceed this way. The reason is that anything you say today can be twisted, taken out of context and used against you, and we don't want to give them anything they can use. If they think they have a case against you, let them prove it. Make them go look for evidence. Otherwise, they can go to hell, okay?"

She took a deep breath and let it out. "That makes sense, I guess. I'm sorry I yelled at you, my nerves are shot." She gave me a wan smile and I patted her arm.

Then Becca gave me a puzzled look. "But why not just leave, what's the point of staying but not answering their questions?"

"So we can find out what their game is," I answered. "Just remember, give them no reaction to anything. Got it?"

"Got it."

We drove the short distance to the state attorney's office in silence, each of us absorbed in our own thoughts. I was also mentally preparing myself for a showdown with Nick Dimitropoulos. If Becca stuck to the script, everything would turn out fine, but I didn't trust Nick. Dirty tricks were his specialty, and criminal law definitely wasn't mine.

We were ushered into a drab room where everything was brown, the carpet, the table, the chairs. Even the walls were beige. It looked like a room where hope went to die. We sat down and waited. It was a good fifteen minutes before the prince of snark, himself, strolled into the room.

"Good morning, Ms. Quinn, *Mrs.* Solomon." He was already starting his head games with Becca.

"Hello, Nick." I said. Becca nodded, but said nothing.

"Thank you for coming in," he said. "I've asked you here to make a statement regarding Joe Solomon's death. Everything you say will be recorded and may be used against you in a court of law. Do you understand Mrs. Solomon?"

Becca nodded again.

"You have to answer audibly, for the record."

"Yes," she said. "I understand."

"I see you have chosen to bring counsel with you, is that correct?"

"Yes."

"Please state the name of your counsel."

"Jamie Quinn."

"Please state your name and address."

"Rebecca Solomon. 3700 S. 37th Court, Hollywood Hills, Florida."

"Do you believe your husband committed suicide, Mrs. Solomon?"

"I don't know," she answered. I glared at her and she flinched. She was off script already!

"Do you believe your husband was murdered?"

"I refuse to answer on the grounds that it might incriminate me," she said, as if each word burned her mouth on the way out.

"Interesting," Nick commented.

"Do you know of anyone who might've killed your husband?"

"I refuse to answer on the grounds that it might incriminate me." Becca was very pale and squirming in her seat.

Nick stopped to rifle through his papers, as if he had all the time in the world.

"Did you have any reason to kill your husband?"

"I refuse to answer on the grounds that it might incriminate me."

"Weren't you in the middle of a nasty divorce when your husband died?"

"I refuse to answer on the grounds that it might incriminate me." Tears were flowing down Becca's face.

Nick switched gears.

"Isn't it true you have a prescription for sleeping pills?" he asked.

"I refuse to answer on the grounds that it might incriminate me."

"Are you aware that your husband Joe died of an overdose of alcohol and sleeping pills?"

"I refuse to answer on the grounds that it might incriminate me." Becca was starting to sway unsteadily in her seat.

Nick put his papers down and looked Becca in the eyes. "Do you have any idea how your sleeping pills ended up at Joe's house? *In an aspirin bottle?*"

Becca let out a shriek before crying out, "Oh my God! No-no-no!"

And then she fainted.

CHAPTER 25

I CAUGHT BECCA BEFORE SHE FELL OUT OF HER CHAIR, while Nick's assistant ran to get some smelling salts. As soon as she cracked one open, the powerful ammonia smell permeated the small room, sending me into a coughing fit. One wave of that miniature stink bomb under her nose was enough to revive Becca and she sat up, looking dazed, as if she couldn't remember where she was.

I glared at Nick. *"We're done here.* And I hope you're proud of yourself!"

"You know what your problem is, Quinn?" he asked. "You take everything so personally. Are you sure she's not your cousin?"

"I may take things personally, but at least I haven't lost my compassion. Once you lose that, Nick, what's left?"

"A damn good attorney, that's what," he said, and walked out of the room.

I helped Becca to her feet and once she was steady, guided her to the door. Before we left the building, I insisted she drink some water from the water fountain in the hall. Thankfully, we

made it to the parking lot without incident and I settled her
into the passenger seat.

"Are you feeling better now?" I asked, as I started the car.

"Yes, thanks. I don't remember what happened, though."

"The state attorney was asking you questions when you
fainted. Do you remember what he asked you that made you so
upset?" I knew it was a risky question, but at least she was in a
safe place.

"I'm sorry, Jamie, I don't."

"It's okay, don't worry about it," I said, wondering whether
Becca was being sincere. She seemed to be. Either she was an
extraordinary actor, or she had the capacity to instantly block
out traumatic events. Either way, it was curious. Sometimes, I
regretted not majoring in psychology; it would have been fasci-
nating to learn how the mind works.

I didn't feel comfortable letting Becca drive, so I convinced
her to let me drop her at home; she and Charlie could pick up
her car later. I walked her into her house and then took Charlie
aside to tell him Becca had fainted and to keep an eye on her.
As usual, he was amiable and agreeable and said he would take
care of her. I wondered what it would take to rile Charlie up,
but I couldn't picture it. Nobody could be that calm all the
time, not even Mother Teresa or the Dalai Lama.

On my drive back to the office, I called Duke.

"Hey there," I said, "I just left the State Attorney's office
with Becca and something interesting happened I thought you
should know about."

"Ain't life strange? I've got something to tell you, too. Ladies
first."

I described the bizarre episode I'd witnessed and asked him
what he thought it meant.

"Well, it sounds like our girl Becca's feeling guilty about
those sleeping pills in the aspirin bottle. But it also sounds like

she was surprised to hear about it. I'd say that was good news, except for the other thing, her black-out. I think it's possible she's the killer, but doesn't remember a thing!"

"But when would she have had the opportunity to kill Joe?"

"That's what I was going to tell ya, Jamie. I went to Joe's place, which is a fancy condo with all kinds of security and a guard sitting in the lobby to check in visitors. Me and him got to talkin', you know how it goes, and he shows me the list of Joe's visitors. Turns out Charlie Santoro paid Joe a visit the day he died. But what was even more interesting was the other visitor, a woman. According to the guard, this same woman visited every Thursday morning and stayed a while, if you catch my drift."

"Wow! What was her name?"

"You're gonna love this--she *said her name was Jamie Quinn!*"

"What the hell? You're joking, right?"

"I wish I was, Darlin'. I asked him to describe this mystery lady and it didn't sound anything like you."

"Of course it wasn't me!" I was furious that someone would use my name like that.

Duke laughed. "You're funny when you're mad."

"Come on, Duke, you're killing me. Who was she?"

"I hate to tell you this, Jamie, I really do, but it was Becca."

CHAPTER 26

I GASPED IN DISBELIEF--BECCA AND JOE WERE SLEEPING together! I couldn't get over it.

"Talk about your love/hate relationship," I said.

"There's no figurin' out people," Duke said, "So I stopped trying a long time ago. One thing's true though, when it comes to sex or money, all bets are off."

I had parked at my office, but stayed in the car. My mind was racing.

"Do we know why Charlie went over there, because he told me he hadn't seen Joe."

"Yeah, the guard said he brought a bunch of kid stuff over and gave it to Joe in the lobby. He didn't go up to Joe's apartment," Duke said.

"That must've been stuff for the Friday visit with the kids, but he still lied about it. And, from what you're saying, it seems like Becca had lots of opportunities to stash an aspirin bottle full of Ambien at Joe's place."

"Yup."

"But then why was she so upset when Nick asked about the aspirin bottle?" I asked.

"Guilty conscience? I'm just guessing."

I confessed to Duke that I didn't know what to do next. Becca was my client and I had an ethical obligation not to act against her best interests. But, with the way I felt about her now, my only choice was to withdraw from the case and cut all ties. I'd say we had some irreconcilable differences, for sure.

"Well," Duke said, "I hope you don't mind if I stay on the case. I was hired to find evidence that might clear Becca, and I'm not through looking. I haven't earned my money yet, is what I'm saying."

"Of course you should stay on. And I'm sure Susan Doyle will still agree to represent Becca, if and when charges are filed. Jeez, if she only represented innocent people, she'd have to close her doors. You know, Duke, Susan could be a great source of business for you. She specifically asked for you on this case."

"She did? Well, hallelujah for that!"

"A word of advice?"

"Yeah, what?"

"Don't hit on her, and don't let her know you conduct all your business from a bar," I joked.

"Gotcha!" He laughed. "And thanks for the business. I knew one day you'd introduce me to all the hot lady lawyers in town."

"Bye, Duke. And good luck."

"I think I'm going to need it," he said.

I felt awful about Becca, and not because she may have killed her husband, but because I'd been duped. I'd worked so hard for her, and the whole time she'd been lying to me. I really hated to think that Nick was right, that I take things too personally, and that my sense of compassion is a hindrance. To be honest, I didn't know what to think anymore.

I spent the rest of the afternoon in a fog, at my desk,

drafting pleadings, writing letters and returning phone calls. I even ate at my desk, ordering food in rather than going out again. I was relieved to see that I had a mediation scheduled for the next day. Playing mediator was actually enjoyable since it amounted to creative problem solving with no preparation required. It was very satisfying to help couples resolve their differences in a civilized way. And not by murdering each other.

CHAPTER 27

FRIDAY MORNING FLEW BY; I WAS SO ENGROSSED IN THE mediation process. These sessions are confidential, so I can't tell you the specifics, but I can tell you that all major issues were resolved in the first half hour. And then it took another five hours to resolve the nitty-gritty stuff. As they say, the devil is in the details.

There's always one thing that jams the process up right at the very end, and it's something that seems stupid to the rest of us. One time it was a DVD collection, another time it was a microwave, this time it was a harp. I've come to realize that it's not the object that matters, it's what it represents. It's a symbol-- of the last concession they will ever make, the last fight they will ever have, the last connection between them. By walking away from that trivial object, they have to face the end of their marriage and all the hopes and dreams they once had together. It's tough.

Now, I know it's not manual labor, but mediation can be pretty exhausting. Although I love it, I couldn't do it every day. That's why I spent the rest of the afternoon goofing off, surfing the Internet and shooting the breeze with my office mates. I decided to research horseback riding so I could get a leg up (ha ha) on my big date with Kip, which was less than twenty-four hours away. What I was looking for was tips on how to do it, what I found was this:

The most common injury is falling from the horse, followed by being kicked, trampled, and bitten. About 3 out of 4 injuries are due to falling, broadly defined. A broad definition of falling often includes being crushed and being thrown from the horse, but when reported separately each of these mechanisms may be more common than being kicked.

Thanks Wikipedia!

I know I said I wanted to leave my comfort zone, but this isn't exactly what I had in mind. I thought it was understood that I'm never going to jump out of a perfectly good plane; I'm never going to dive into the ocean with a canister of oxygen on my back just to see the pretty fishes; and I'm never going on a safari where I can be eaten by wild animals.

I was starting to freak myself out, but then, I got a grip. After all, I wasn't going to a rodeo; I was going to a county park. If it were a dangerous activity, they wouldn't have horseback riding there. (Think of the liability issues!) And I knew Kip would keep me safe. He was the lifeguard who'd saved the most kids from drowning at Castaway Island, so, keeping an uncoordinated friend from falling off a horse would be easy for him. I'm glad I have a rational side, because if the wimpy, scaredy-cat side ever took over, I'd spend the rest of my life hiding under the covers. Seriously.

I had an appointment at five for a pedicure (so my toes would look pretty right before the horse trampled them), and I was getting ready to leave when Grace called.

"Hey Gracie, what's new?"

"Jamie, I just got off the phone with my friend at the

Consulate, and you're not going to believe this. Your father has a pending visa application to come to the U.S.! It's been pending for over two years, but still, he has one."

"That's incredible! But, how is that possible? I thought only a U.S. citizen could petition on behalf of their relatives. Someone would've had to apply on his behalf...right?"

"Someone did, Jamie."

"Who was it?"

"His wife."

CHAPTER 28

I SAT THERE, HOLDING THE PHONE. I DIDN'T KNOW WHAT to say. I'd been so worried about my father's reaction to learning he had a daughter that I hadn't considered he might already have a family, one that was complete without me.

"Jamie, honey? Are you there?" Grace asked.

"Yeah, I'm here. Sorry, I was thinking."

"Well, it's a big surprise, but it's still good news, right?"

"Definitely," I said. "It's excellent news."

"There's more. Your dad's wife lives in Miami. Her name is Ana Maria Suarez, I have her number. You could call her."

"Um, I'm not sure if that's a wise idea. I'd hate to break up my dad's marriage before I even got to talk to him."

"Good point. Why don't you think about it and, in the meantime, I'll send you her contact information. Okay?"

"Okay. Thanks so much, Grace!"

"Anything for you. Hey, if you're not busy next Saturday morning, do you want to volunteer with me at a food bank?"

"Sure, of course," I said. Grace was such a do-gooder.

"Great! We'll figure out the details next week. Have fun with Kip tomorrow, I want a full report, you hear?"

I laughed. "I'll call you from the emergency room."

"Such an optimist," Grace said.

"Just a realist."

After we hung up, I sat at my desk, lost in reverie. Everything had gotten so complicated lately, and nothing was what it seemed. I'd thought Becca was a victim, and now it looked like she was the bad guy. I'd thought my father had abandoned me, and it turned out he didn't even know I existed. I'd thought I could reach out to him if I found him, and now I had to consider his wife's feelings. I'd thought he might need my help, but now it seemed like he had everything under control. Maybe I should just stop thinking so much. Maybe I was just tired from my mediation. Maybe a nice, relaxing pedicure was just what I needed.

It turned out that it was.

It was Saturday morning and I was trying to decide what one wears to go horseback riding. After perusing the limited selections my closet had to offer, I opted for a short-sleeved shirt, jeans and sneakers. I was way too wired and excited to eat, so I drank some coffee and pocketed a granola bar for later. It was only 11:30 and we weren't meeting at the park until one, so I had some time to kill. Suddenly I remembered that Joe's funeral had been that morning, which made me think about their little girls. Poor things!

My cell started ringing, which snapped me out of it. Why was Duke calling? We'd just spoken the day before.

"Have I got a story for you!" he said, as soon as I picked up.

"Hello to you, too."

"Man, Jamie, that was a hell of a funeral!"

"*You went to Joe's funeral?* Why would you do that?" I was flabbergasted.

"I'm an investigator, aren't I? All of Joe's and Becca's friends and family were in one place--can you think of a better way for me to get some answers?"

"I guess that makes sense in a weird way. Crashing funerals seems a little over the top to me, but, hey, that's why I'm not an investigator."

"So, listen to this, I'm chatting with Joe's friends before the service--they think I'm his cousin from Louisiana--and they tell me some interesting things..."

"Go on."

"They say the reason Becca and Joe split up was that Joe was sick of her pill popping. She really loves her mother's little helpers--Xanax, Valium, Ambien, you name it. Whatever she could con her doctor into giving her."

"That would explain her tendency to turn into a zombie, but why is it important?"

"I'll tell you why, young lady. Because even after she told Joe she'd quit the pills, she kept taking them, and she didn't want him to know."

"So?"

"So, she would hide them like a squirrel in winter. I think I know where one of her hiding place was...see if you can guess."

"No!! An aspirin bottle!"

"Bingo!"

"So, when Joe got home Thursday night after drinking too much, he took two Ambien thinking they were aspirin, and never woke up."

"Oh-my-God! But we still don't know how the bottle got there."

"No, we don't."

"Wow! I'm blown away by that. What else did his friends say?" I asked.

"Well, they said boyfriend Charlie had an alcoholic mother and that he always had to pick up the pieces after her."

"That explains a lot. He's co-dependent--that's why he takes care of Becca and never complains."

"Yup. Now, ask me what happened next." Duke said, suddenly serious.

"What happened next?"

"Becca went nuts--screaming and crying and carrying on, not making any sense, and then she collapsed and someone called 911. When the paramedics got there, she went nuts again. They had to sedate her to get her into the ambulance. I heard they were gonna Baker Act her, whatever that is."

"That's an involuntary psych evaluation where they can hold you for up to 72 hours. What do you think's going on with her--is it guilt, or is it grief?"

"There's no tellin'. Could also be mental problems or drug abuse. Or all of the above."

"What a mess! So, where are her kids now?" I asked.

"They went home with Joe's parents. I already called Susan Doyle and told her what happened. She asked me to keep digging around, try to find out how the aspirin bottle ended up at Joe's house."

"Makes sense. I wish I could be there when Nick hears his prime suspect is in the psych ward! I'm a sick person, aren't I? Don't answer that. Anyway, Duke, you're certainly earning your money, keep up the good work."

"Thanks, Darlin'. I appreciate it. So, what are you doing on this beautiful day?"

"Believe it or not, I'm going horseback riding. I have a date."

CHAPTER 29

ALTHOUGH T.Y. PARK IS ONE OF MY FAVORITE PARKS, Tradewinds Park is really the jewel in the crown. At almost five times the size of T.Y., it's one of Broward County's largest parks and has the most to offer. Besides the usual playgrounds, shelters, and fishing, Tradewinds has a model steam train, a flying disc golf course, an educational farm, and *Butterfly World*, a walk-through tropical garden with thousands of live butterflies, an insect museum, a lorikeet encounter, botanical gardens, and several aviaries, including the largest free-flight hummingbird aviary in the country. And, let's not forget the horse stables, where I was now headed.

I was excited about seeing Kip, but worried that it might be awkward after all these years. While we were still those teenagers who had fallen in love, at the same time, we were strangers. It's harder when you have a history together because you're not the same people you used to be, no matter how much you wish you were. Does that make any sense?

But all that went out the window the minute I saw Kip standing next to the stables, the wind playing with his hair as he stroked the mane of a beautiful black horse. He was wearing worn-looking jeans, low-cut boots and a Rolling Stones t-shirt, the same shirt he'd bought when he took me to see the Stones in Miami all those years ago. We had such a great time at that concert! How about that Kip? He was scoring points with me already, and he hadn't even said hello.

When he saw me, he gave me a big grin.

"Hey there, Jamie. How ya' doing? Ready to tear up the trails?"

"I'm ready to tear up something." I said with a laugh.

"Okay, let's get started. Would you like to meet your horse? This is Star. She's very gentle and knows the trail backwards and forwards".

"How do I make friends with her, bribe her with food? Chocolate usually works for me."

Kip smiled and his brown eyes lit up. "I'll have to remember that. Now, this is how you introduce yourself to a horse. It's called the 'horseman's handshake'. Offer her the back of your hand to smell and then pet her on the nose or the head."

I approached the horse nervously (of course) and did as Kip said. Once she nuzzled her nose against my hand, I felt myself relax. Then Kip went over the basics: how to mount a horse; where to put your feet in the stirrups (only a third of the way in, so you don't get hung up in case of a fall!); how to hold the reins (not too much slack); and how to sit in the saddle (your shoulder, hip and heel should be aligned). He explained that to make your horse move forward, you squeeze with your calves, and to make your horse halt or slow down, you sit deep in the saddle and apply pressure with the reins. You can also say "whoa" (that part I knew). To turn your horse, you pull the left or right rein out to the side and apply pressure with your outside leg.

"Is that everything I need to know?" I asked. My stomach

was full of butterflies, and not the kind they had at Butterfly World.

"One more thing," Kip said. "Don't forget to breathe, Jamie, or you'll pass out and fall off the horse!" He put his arm around my shoulders and gave me a squeeze.

That made me feel much better. And I couldn't help but notice, Kip smelled as wonderful as I remembered.

"There's a quote by Thornton Wilder I like," Kip said. "*When you're safe at home you wish you were having an adventure; when you're having an adventure you wish you were safe at home.*"

I laughed. "I love it! That's exactly how I feel."

I practiced getting on and off the horse and went through the drill of how to go, stop, slow down and steer. Then I waited with Star while Kip went to the stable to get his horse, a striking reddish-brown colt named Webster. Webster seemed a little feistier than Star, like he couldn't wait to get on the trail. In other words, the perfect horse for Kip.

It took an hour to complete the trail that looped through a shady, wooded area. We were surrounded on both sides by live oak, mahogany, and gumbo limbo trees, with their red, peeling bark. No wonder they were called 'tourist trees'. Some of the trees were buried under winding vines of strangler figs that were literally choking them to death. They looked surreal, like a weird piece of modern art.

My favorite plant by far was the wild coffee, which seemed to be everywhere. Even if we'd missed seeing their signature red berries and shiny leaves in the underbrush, we couldn't miss the delicious coffee aroma following us down the trail. Kip told me the Latin name for wild coffee was *Psychotria nervosa*, and that birds and wildlife liked to eat the berries. That cracked me up. I said I'd love to see some overly-caffeinated wildlife.

He laughed. "If you think that's funny, you need to go to Butterfly World and see the drunk butterflies."

"Kip, you're making that up!"

"I'd never lie about drunk butterflies! Those crazy things leave their fruit until it ferments, and then they eat it and fly around drunk. It's hilarious! Luckily, there aren't any predators inside the Butterfly Garden or they'd be goners."

You may be wondering why I haven't talked about the actual horseback riding yet. That's because it was relaxing and easy, and not scary at all. I couldn't have asked for a better horse than Star. Or a better guide than Kip. As we ambled along, we caught each other up on the people we used to know, our jobs and our families. Kip was very upset to hear my mom had died; the two of them used to get along so well. Happily, Kip's parents were alive and well, living in Sacramento where they owned a medical equipment company. His older brother, Chuck, was in New York City, managing an off-Broadway theatre company. I didn't tell Kip about my search for my dad; it just seemed like too much for a first date.

We were coming up on the end of the trail when Kip gave me a look that said he was up to no good. He yelled, "Hang on, Jamie!" and then swatted Star in the rear. She started to pick up the pace and before I knew what had happened, we were both flying down the trail. It was terrifying! Also exciting and fun. The horses came to a stop on their own at the end of the trail. By then, I was out of breath and I didn't think my behind would ever recover from that bruising saddle.

"I'm going to kill you, Kip!" I laughed, "If I ever figure out how to get off this horse."

He was laughing so hard. "That doesn't give me much incentive to help you, now does it?"

After he'd helped me down, he pulled me into his arms and gave me a kiss. I gave him one back.

"This checking out parks with you is fun," he said, as he stroked my hair.

"Glad you thought of it," I agreed, with a smile. Yes, I was *very* glad.

"What do you think about going to Quiet Waters Park with me next Saturday?"

Quiet Waters sounded tame enough, so I said I would love to. Then he gave me that look again, and I knew I was in trouble.

"Excellent! We can try out the ski rixen."

"I'm not sure I like the sound of that. What's a ski rixen?"

"It's where you stand on water skis and a cable pulls you around a one mile course. There are jumps and slides that you can do along the way. It's a blast! Trust me, Jamie--you're going to love it!"

I guess I would just to have to trust him

CHAPTER 30

I was flying high after my date with Kip, so much so that I didn't mind at all when I couldn't sleep. Not sleeping is part of who I am, unfortunately, but that night it gave me a chance to relive our time together, analyzing every word and gesture. I couldn't stop smiling. It was unbelievable that I would run into him the one day I decided to exercise, and even more unbelievable that he would ask me out. Oprah recommends keeping a gratitude journal and I always meant to start one. Now, I know exactly what I'd write in it.

My insomnia also gave me time to think about my father. I was so close to reaching him, but I just couldn't bring myself to contact his wife. She had to be going through so much already, with him in Nicaragua and her here, and having to fight for a visa to bring him to the U.S. The last thing she needed was a woman claiming to be his long-lost daughter to add to her problems. I'd have to find him on my own--well, with Grace's help-- but not through his wife. It just didn't seem right to me.

Luckily, it was Sunday, so I could sleep in. I planned on a leisurely brunch, followed by some intense house-cleaning. For a small house, it sure piled up a lot of dirt, not to mention cat hair. I dragged myself out of bed around noon and made some coffee. I was about to scramble some eggs and whip up some cheese grits when Grace called.

"Tell me everything," she demanded.

"No 'Good morning'? What would Miss Manners say?"

"She'd say, 'It's afternoon, Princess, time to get up.'"

"Hey, I've been up for a good ten minutes already."

"Whatever. How was your date? You didn't spend the night in the emergency room, I take it. Did you spend it somewhere more interesting? Do tell."

"No, Grace," I said, as I boiled the water for my grits. "I was home last night, although I did have company in bed. Unfortunately, it was just the cat."

"Well, did you have fun? Did you make another date? Come on, Jamie, you're killing me!"

I laughed. "Yes and yes. I had an amazing time and we're going out again next Saturday. Kip's really great." I hesitated.

"I hear a 'but' coming," Grace said.

"Well, it's just that...how do I say this? He's so interesting and I'm so boring! Kip's like 'Mr. Adventure', always looking for a mountain to climb, while I'm happy spending the day at Barnes and Noble. He's going to figure it out pretty soon."

Grace started laughing so hard, she had to put the phone down. "Jamie, honey, if he didn't figure that out yesterday, he's never going to."

"Figure out that I'm boring?" I was feeling a little insulted, even though I'd said it first.

"No, that you're the opposite of adventurous."

"I guess you're right," I said. "There's no hiding the real me. But next Saturday we're going to *another* park, this time to water-ski!"

Grace chuckled. "I definitely need pictures of that. Maybe for your next date, you can take him to Barnes and Noble."

"Very funny. Do you think I can learn to water ski by watching YouTube? If not, I'm in trouble. Seriously."

"You'll be fine, I'm the one who's in trouble. I have that big trial tomorrow. I think I'm ready, but who knows?"

"Just use your 'voice of reason' and the judge will have to rule for you." I finished scrambling the eggs and then sprinkled cheese on the grits.

"It's a *jury* trial and my client is so obnoxious, everyone hates him. Including me. I wish I didn't have to put him on the stand at all."

"Well, here's what I'd do. Put him on the stand right away and get it over with. Then, finish with your most charming witness and the jury will forget all about him. First impressions don't matter as much as the last one."

"I like it!" Grace said. "Now I just need to find a charming witness."

Before we hung up, I wished her luck. She said if I didn't hear from her after the trial, it meant she lost and she was rethinking her career choices. Like, maybe she'd move to Alaska and train for the Iditarod.

I ate my brunch on the patio, enjoying the mid-day heat as well as the light breeze that hinted of fall. Weather changes are subtle in south Florida, but we appreciate them; unlike the tourists, who think it's summer here year-round. Another advantage to sitting outside was I could ignore my dirty house, or pretend it was someone else's.

My phone buzzed with a text message and I tried to resist looking at it. I wish I could break the phone habit, but I can't-- I'm totally addicted. If there were a twelve-step program available, I'd think about doing it, but, honestly, I'd rather give up chocolate than my phone. I waited a whole twenty seconds before I broke down and read the text. It was from Duke.

You still on a date, Darlin'? You go, girl!!

If I were on a date, do you really think I'd be texting you?

Sure, if you needed my expert advice.

Never gonna happen.

Okay, but that offer doesn't expire. Hey, do you know where Charlie Santoro is? I can't find him.

No clue. At Becca's house? I texted.

Nope, she's still in the psych ward. And Charlie doesn't answer his phone.

Wish I could help you, Duke.

Me too. I get the feeling he knows more than he's telling.

You could be right.

Aren't I always?

You're a legend in your own mind. Got to go now.

Adios, Ms. Esquire.

Duke was right--if anyone knew how that aspirin bottle ended up at Joe's place, it was probably Charlie. Since he'd been living at Becca's for the past few months, I wondered where he would've gone, but it wasn't my problem anymore. What *was* my problem was a house desperately in need of cleaning.

I was just about to break out the mop and the vacuum cleaner when my neighbor Sandy came over and invited me to go to the Yellow Green Farmer's Market. The thought of fresh produce, exotic juice drinks, the Amish cheese booth (with free samples!) and live mellow music was too much to resist. I closed the door to my dirty house and it was out of sight, out of mind for the rest of the day.

CHAPTER 31

Monday morning found me back at work, but not exactly working. I was off to a slow start--surfing the web, reading the news, checking out Facebook--basically, anything I could do to avoid work. I'm a master procrastinator, but, like any acquired skill, it took me years of practice.

I was enjoying my early morning solitude when Lisa burst into my office, clearly distraught.

"Jamie, there's a crazy homeless guy in the lobby and he won't leave! He said he has to talk to you. What should I do? Call the police?"

"It's alright, Lisa, I'll go see what he wants. Why don't you wait here?"

I was a little nervous, I'll admit. Being a divorce lawyer isn't the safest job in the world, especially considering that two of my colleagues had been killed by angry litigants in the past few years. There's a reason metal detectors had been installed in every courthouse, it was necessary.

I peered into the lobby and saw a disheveled young guy

pacing back and forth, as if he couldn't stand still. I didn't recognize him until l he turned to face me.

"Charlie? Oh my God, what happened to you?"

He stopped pacing, but still had a wild look in his eyes.

"I need to talk to you. Please, can I talk to you?"

"Sure, Charlie, but how about I get you a bottle of water and a snack first? Maybe some coffee?"

He shook his head.

"Then why don't we sit right here and you can tell me what's on your mind. Nobody will bother us."

We sat in adjoining arm chairs and I waited, but Charlie didn't say a word. He just stared at his shoes. I didn't know which topics were safe, or what he could possibly want from me, so I didn't say anything. I would've given him money for food, or referred him to a mental health provider, if that's what he wanted. It sure looked like what he needed.

"So...what's going on, Charlie?" I asked, after several minutes had gone by.

Once he started talking, the words flew out of his mouth. "I loved her so much", he said, locking his eyes on my face. "I did everything for her, but she didn't care. No matter what I did, it wasn't good enough, *I* was never good enough. She used me, like she used everyone!"

I wasn't sure if he meant Becca or his mother.

"She used you, too, Jamie," Charlie stated flatly.

Okay, he was talking about Becca.

"What happened?" I asked.

Suddenly, Charlie was sobbing uncontrollably and it made him look like a little boy. I was in familiar territory now; if there's one thing I'm good at, it's comforting crying people. I patted him gently on the back.

"It's alright, Charlie," I said in a soothing voice. "Everything's going to be okay."

I saw Lisa peek around the corner and motioned for her to bring a bottle of water, which she quickly did.

Charlie took a sip of water and then, in a ragged voice, continued, "It was Saturday--before the funeral--and Becca was crying. She told me she'd never stopped loving Joe and that I'd never be as good as him. Then she started screaming at me to leave because she couldn't stand to look at me!" Tears were streaming unchecked down Charlie's face.

I nodded sympathetically. "That must've been rough. Where have you been sleeping since Saturday, Charlie?" I asked.

"In my car." At that, he started rocking back and forth and I thought he might pass out, but he didn't. Then, in a voice so low he could've been talking to himself, he said, "I just wanted to make her happy. I tried so hard...and I never told anyone..."

Ah! Here we go. "Told anyone what, Charlie?"

"About her pills. She took so many pills! When I threw them out, she'd just go buy more. She said she'd stop, but it was a lie."

"Do you know if she hid her sleeping pills in an aspirin bottle?"

Charlie nodded.

"Did Joe take them with him?"

When Charlie nodded again, he looked like he was barely keeping it together.

"Was it an accident?" I asked.

No response.

"Charlie?" I was sure now that Becca had slipped those pills to Joe. All that guilt and remorse had eaten away at her until she'd had a major meltdown at the funeral.

Charlie took a deep breath. When he spoke, it was barely above a whisper.

"It wasn't supposed to kill him," Charlie said, "Just mess him up a little, so Becca could get custody of the girls. He shouldn't have threatened her like that! I tried to talk to him, but he wouldn't stop, he just went on and on. It was his own fault, he did it to himself."

"And that's why Becca did it?" I asked.

Charlie looked up at me with dead eyes.

"No, Jamie. That's why I did it."

CHAPTER 32

I SAT THERE IN STUNNED SILENCE. ALTHOUGH MANY people have told me their secrets over the years (sometimes while I'm at the grocery store minding my own business), nobody had ever made a confession like that. I don't know why Charlie chose to tell me (I like to think it's because I'm a good listener), but it did put me in a quandary.

What was I supposed to do with this information? Call Susan Doyle? I sure as hell wasn't going to call Nick Dimitropoulos. I briefly considered calling the Florida Bar ethics hotline, but decided against it. What would I say? That my former client's ex-boyfriend just told me he accidentally killed a former friend who was also his ex-girlfriend's estranged husband in order to help her get custody? I doubt that there's a rule to cover that, or even an Attorney General opinion. Finally, I simply asked Charlie.

"What are you going to do now?"

"Turn myself in," he said solemnly without hesitation.

"Why?" I asked, "I mean--"

"I know what I did and I have to own it. And I don't want Becca to take the blame."

"After all she's done to you?" I was incredulous.

"Yes," Charlie said, and he stood up to leave. We shook hands and he thanked me for seeing him. He looked so lost, it was really heartbreaking. As he was about to walk out the door, he turned around and said, "I know it doesn't make any sense, but I still love her." And then he was gone.

All of us make our share of poor decisions. Most of the time, it turns out alright and nothing bad happens. Then there's Charlie, son of an alcoholic mother, destined to end up with a woman as messed up as his mother, and he makes a really poor decision. He slips Joe sleeping pills that look like aspirin. If Joe hadn't been drinking, the pills wouldn't have killed him, but he was, and they did, and now Charlie had to live with that.

When I told Duke about Charlie, he was sympathetic. Since Duke also can't resist helping a damsel in distress, he could relate. The difference is that Duke wouldn't kill anyone. At least, I don't think he would. Nah, of course he wouldn't.

Susan Doyle took the news in stride, of course. When I asked her about Becca, Susan said she'd been placed in a 30 day drug rehab program. She also told me that the psych eval indicated Becca had possible multiple personality disorder, which I thought explained a lot. She said an insanity defense would've been a slam dunk. As for Charlie, she thought he would be charged with negligent homicide. She said it could've been a lot worse.

After I hung up with Susan, Lisa popped her head into my office to ask me a question. She said she was so impressed with how I'd handled Charlie that she was considering switching to mental health counseling when she went back to school. She wanted my opinion.

"Do you think it will make you happy?" I asked.

She nodded and smiled.

"Then you should definitely do it!" I said, hopeful that she wouldn't feel like crying anymore.

I had one more phone call to make. Actually, I didn't have to, I just wanted to.

"Nick Dimitropoulos here."

"I hate to say I told you so--"

"That's a lie, Quinn. You love to say it. Why else would you be calling me?"

I laughed. "I *do* love to say it, especially to you. You got the wrong guy again, Nick! How does it feel? Maybe you should buy a Magic 8 Ball so you can ask it for advice."

"Maybe you should ask yourself how you keep getting in the middle of murder cases," he tossed right back at me.

"I do ask myself that. And I honestly don't know."

"Quit caring so much. That might do the trick," he chuckled.

"I'll see what I can do," I said. "In the meantime, if you need empathy lessons, you know where to find me."

"Yeah, that'll happen, Quinn. See you in another year."

"I sure hope not, but don't take it personally."

"I never do," he said.

CHAPTER 33

I DON'T WANT YOU TO THINK FOR A MINUTE THAT WITH everything else going on, I had stopped obsessing about my own stuff. Au contraire! The debate teams competing in my head were tireless, they never took a break. *Should I contact my dad's wife? What if I ruined my one chance to meet him? Should I be worried about my upcoming date with Kip? What if he realized I was a boring homebody? And what's behind door number 2? Is it a goat or a brand new car?* Those guys loved to argue, but they never had any answers for me.

As far as contacting my dad's wife, Ana Maria Suarez, I kept going back and forth, making lists of pros and cons until I finally just went with my gut. I couldn't picture myself contacting her, so I decided to wait until Grace got me his address in Nicaragua. Then I would write to him.

As for Kip, that problem solved itself. On Friday night, Kip called to tell me that the forecast for Saturday was thunder-showers, so we couldn't go water skiing. I was crushed because I thought he was canceling our date, or at least postponing it, but that was not the case.

"So, Jamie," he said, "how would you like to go to Coral Cliffs instead? At least we wouldn't get wet."

I knew exactly what that was--it was an indoor rock climbing gym! There was no way on this planet I was going to climb a wall (not that I could've anyway) because I was terrified of heights. It was time to introduce Kip to the real me.

"Kip, I really want to spend time with you and it doesn't matter where we go, but I have to be honest--I don't do heights. No way, no how. It's all I can do to stand on my kitchen counter to reach the top shelf. But I'm happy to watch you climb."

He started laughing and it was the most beautiful sound in the world.

"Now I remember! When we used to have diving contests at Castaway Island, you were always the judge. I'm sorry, Jamie, that was pretty inconsiderate of me. I want to hang out with you, not terrorize you! What would you like to do?"

I laughed too. "While I'm being honest about my character flaws, I have to tell you that, in general, I'm kind of a big chicken. Also, I'm not very athletic. And I trip a lot, but only because I'm not paying attention. Now, do you still want to go out with me?"

"More than ever!" Kip said. "How can I resist a girl with so many fine qualities?"

I couldn't stop smiling. "I'm going out on a limb here, but how would you feel about seeing a movie? It can be an action movie, I love seeing *other* people be daredevils."

"Only if we can go to dinner and talk first. Who knows? Maybe you'll reveal some more deep dark secrets."

"Deal. I'd better think of some before then," I said. "Or maybe you could reveal some of yours. Now, that would be interesting."

"Only if I made them up," Kip said. "Pick you up at six?"

"Perfect! I can't wait. Oh, and I'm a vegetarian--pescatarian, actually--I forgot to mention that."

"Okay, no Brazilian steakhouses then. Got it."

"But it's okay if you want to eat meat in front of me, I don't mind."

"So, as long as I don't make you climb a wall or eat meat, we're good?" he laughed.

"Yes, we're very good," I said.

"You're very good," he said in a low voice that gave me goose bumps. "See you tomorrow, Jamie."

"Good night, Kip."

This was what happy felt like. I'd almost forgotten.

CHAPTER 34

ALTHOUGH I WAS LOOKING FORWARD TO VOLUNTEERING AT the Food Bank the next morning, I was relieved that it wasn't until ten o'clock, so I could stay in bed a while longer. For some reason, the only restful sleep I ever got was early mornings. I told you I was weird.

I heard Grace honking her horn, but ignored it, incorporating the sound into my dream instead. It wasn't until she pounded on the front door that I finally woke up. Damn it! My bizarre sleep habits were so irritating. I threw on a robe, let her in without a word and immediately marched into the bathroom where I hurriedly brushed my teeth, washed my face and tamed my bed-head the best I could.

"Sorry," I said in a mumble, as I threw on some clothes. "No sleep."

"It sure seemed like you were sleeping when I honked." She made a face at me, then went into the kitchen and poured me a glass of juice. After rummaging through the cabinets and finding nothing, she grabbed a banana off the counter, and said, "You're slowing me down, woman, let's go already."

I woke up on the drive to the Broward Outreach Center. As we drove, Grace explained that this was a homeless shelter for women and children, which also had a food bank. They were always looking for volunteers to sort and organize the food bank, but they also needed volunteers at the shelter, including people to help kids with their homework. We talked about maybe doing that another day, although my math skills were pretty rusty. If you saw my checkbook, you'd understand.

Grace asked if I'd made a decision about Ana Maria Suarez, my dad's wife, and I said I'd decided not to call her. Grace didn't even argue with me, she just dropped it. That was unusual for her, but I figured she'd bring it up again later.

Before we went to work at the food bank, Grace and I were given a tour of the facility and we found it quite impressive. It was 18,000 square feet with 120 beds, including family sleeping rooms so that mothers weren't separated from their children. They also offered life skills classes, education labs, counseling, drug treatment, career services and access to medical facilities for these homeless families.

I'm sure there are lots of people who'd like to help the less fortunate in a hands-on way, but they simply don't know how. What I mean is we rarely come into contact with people who need help unless they are our neighbors, co-workers, friends or family. Volunteering at a homeless shelter or a food bank seemed like an excellent way to lend a hand, and Grace and I vowed to do it more often.

As we organized the pantry into canned goods, rice, pasta, cereals and peanut butter, Grace kept checking her watch and giving me sideways glances. I just ignored her. I figured she'd tell me what was going on when she was ready. At 11:30, she jumped up and left the room without an explanation. Where the heck did she go? Bathroom break? Next thing I know, she comes bouncing back into the room with a kind-looking older blonde woman in tow and they are chatting excitedly. Grace points at me and says, "That's Jamie!"

The woman reaches for my hands and pulls me off the floor into a tight embrace. She is holding me like I'm a life preserver and she's about to jump ship. I have no idea what's going on. She starts crying and murmuring, "mi cariño, mi corazón," and then pulls back to examine my face.

"Dios mio! Look at you--you're identical!" And she starts crying.

"I'm sorry, I don't mean to be rude but, who are you? Identical to whom, exactly?"

"To your father, sweet girl! You look just like him!"

In a daze, I look at Grace who is smiling so hard, her face is surely going to freeze like that.

"Is...this?" I stammer.

"Meet Ana Maria Suarez, the director of the shelter." Grace gives me a wink. It's her best stunt ever.

I turn back to Ana Maria with tears in my eyes. I look at her face and all I see is unconditional love, for me, a total stranger. I give her a fierce hug right back. You can never have too many people to love in this world. Or people who love you back.

Grace is sniffing and wiping her eyes. "Jamie, can you and Ana Maria come with me, please?"

At this point, I'm just doing what I'm told; I doubt that I could say anything coherent anyway. We walk into another room and somehow there's my Aunt Peg, my cousin Adam, and Duke, and they're all clapping and cheering. Grace spins me around and there's a giant monitor on the wall. And on that monitor a man is waving and smiling. *It's my father.* I think my heart is going to explode. He looks much older than he did in the picture Duke gave me, but it's definitely him.

"Hello, Jamie," he says, choking up. "I am so happy to see you that I have no words to express it."

"Me too," I say. I've waited all my life to find my father and all I can say is 'me too.'

"I can't believe it's really you," I manage to say before I burst into tears.

He is emotional, too. "Finding out I have a daughter is like a gift from God, Jamie. We have so much to talk about."

"Yes, we do," I say with a lump in my throat. "Where should we start?"

Dear reader,

We hope you enjoyed reading *The Case of the Killer Divorce*. Please take a moment to leave a review, even if it's a short one. Your opinion is important to us.

Discover more books by Barbara Venkataraman at https://www.nextchapter.pub/authors/barbara-venkataraman

Want to know when one of our books is free or discounted? Join the newsletter at http://eepurl.com/bqqB3H

Best regards,

Barbara Vankataraman and the Next Chapter Team

ABOUT THE AUTHOR

Award-winning author Barbara Venkataraman is an attorney in South Florida where she draws inspiration for her books from the daily headlines. She loves connecting with readers through her books and finds a particular kind of joy in a well-turned phrase. In addition to writing fiction, she co-authored *Accidental Activist: Justice for the Groveland Four* with her son Josh Venkataraman about his successful four-year quest to obtain posthumous pardons for The Groveland Four.

The Case Of The Killer Divorce
ISBN: 978-4-86752-891-4

Published by
Next Chapter
1-60-20 Minami-Otsuka
170-0005 Toshima-Ku, Tokyo
+818035793528

7th August 2021